It slowly dawned on her that they were in bed together and that it felt really good—safe. Secure.

She could feel the tension draining out of her body, leaving her limp in his arms. Within minutes she was asleep.

He lay there for ages listening to the even rhythm of her breathing and soaking up her warmth. It felt so good to lie next to her, but he couldn't stay there, not for the rest of the night—not and retain his sanity.

He eased his arm carefully out from under her neck and tucked the pillow there instead. His thigh was throbbing, his pelvis ached and his lower leg was as heavy as lead. There was no way he was going to get back to sleep, so he went into the kitchen, got a glass of water and shuffled over to the sofa. But all he could think about was how she'd felt snuggled up against his side, and how soft and warm her body had been, and how he wanted to protect her.

That scared the spit out of him.

Double Destiny

The right man for Fran?
When nurse Fran Williams reaches a turning point
in her life she finds herself being offered work assignments
with two very different men—men who will offer Fran
more than a job! She doesn't know it, but they
represent her future happiness.

So which is the right man for Fran?
Is it rich, wealthy, energetic Josh Nicholson—
injured, impatient but gorgeous hero number one?
Or charming, sensual, tender Dr. Xavier Giraud,
the single father who needs a woman
to love him and his children?

Or is there more than one Mr. Right?
Find out and explore Fran's parallel lives
with each of these heroes—this month in
Assignment: Single Man, next month in
Assignment: Single Father from Harlequin Romance®.

DOUBLE DESTINY
There is more than one route to happiness.

**Like to see Fran's introduction
to Josh Nicholson and Xavier Giraud?
Caroline Anderson's prequel
to this intriguing duet is free to read.
Look for DOUBLE DESTINY at www.eHarlequin.com.**

ASSIGNMENT: SINGLE MAN

Caroline Anderson

Double Destiny

TORONTO • NEW YORK • LONDON
AMSTERDAM • PARIS • SYDNEY • HAMBURG
STOCKHOLM • ATHENS • TOKYO • MILAN • MADRID
PRAGUE • WARSAW • BUDAPEST • AUCKLAND

ISBN 0-373-03728-7

ASSIGNMENT: SINGLE MAN

First North American Publication 2002.

Visit us at www.eHarlequin.com

Printed in U.S.A.

CHAPTER ONE

IT WAS the sexy grin that did it. That and those arresting cobalt blue eyes that seemed to spear right through her.

She'd come out of the back office to Reception to tell Jackie she was going for a second interview with Xavier Giraud, but she didn't get a chance. Jackie was no longer alone, and the man in there with her was a man she recognised, a man with a sexy, lopsided grin and the most arresting blue eyes she'd ever seen.

Josh looked up at her, and his smile widened in recognition.

'Well, if it isn't the bodacious Sister Williams,' he said, and Fran suppressed a smile.

'Well, if it isn't the accident-prone Mr Nicholson. It's good to see you alive.'

'Do you two know each other?' Jackie chipped in, clearly agog, and he chuckled.

'Let's just say we met over a red-hot needle a little while ago.'

'Yes. How is the chest?' Fran asked him, and he gave a short, humourless laugh.

'Oh, the chest is fine—it's healed beautifully. Unfortunately, though, the rest of me is lagging behind a little, hence my visit here. I need a nurse.'

His smile challenged her—almost dared her to take the job.

Why it seemed like a dare she couldn't imagine, but for some inexplicable reason it did and her heart was beating a tattoo against her ribs. She forced herself to ignore it.

'Why do you need a nurse?' she asked, ruthlessly sticking to the point. 'If you've been discharged from hospital...'

'I've discharged myself,' he said dryly. 'The consultant didn't quite seem to see eye to eye with me about that, but you can't please all of the people all of the time.'

Fran kept her expression carefully neutral. 'You discharged yourself?'

He nodded, the grin kicking up one side of his mouth in a charming, little-boy appeal that had no business affecting her the way it did. She ignored the flutter in her heart—again—and studied him as he sat there in old jogging bottoms and a sweatshirt, one leg stuck out in front of him, his trousers cut up the side to accommodate the paraphernalia of the external fixator.

His right arm—the same side—was in a cast below the elbow, and his hair had been cropped short, perhaps to stitch a scalp wound? It suited him, she thought, sidetracked again by his lazy good looks and those arresting eyes.

Eyes clouded with pain, she realised. His body must have taken a real hammering.

And yet oddly, as mangled as he was, he still exuded power and confidence as well as an undeniable sex appeal. She dragged her mind back into order.

'So, how long ago exactly did you have this accident?' she asked, eyeing the cast on his arm and the metalwork protruding through his trouser leg with concern.

'Twelve days ago.'

Fran blinked. Could it really only have been twelve days? She remembered the news breaking, just as her world was falling apart. He'd been the only bright spot in a hellish week, and when the accident happened it had been all the more shocking because she'd only just treated him. He'd fallen over a cat and landed in a bin bag full of rubbish, cutting his chest. She'd teased him, and then a few days later he'd nearly died.

Was it really only twelve days ago? It seemed forever, but that was her own personal perspective. In terms of this man's injuries it was probably plenty— unless there was more than his arm and leg involved.

He shrugged, the crooked grin widening. 'Well, apart from the bruised spleen, the split liver and the right femur which had to be pinned, not a lot really. Well, except for the clot on my brain. They had to make a little borehole to get it out. Oh, and there's a crack in my pelvis, apparently.'

Fran felt sick. How many young men had she seen like that—and how many of them had lost their tenuous hold on life? Too many, over and over again, day after day, until she thought she'd go mad. She buried the hideous memories and rolled her eyes.

'You must be out of your mind, discharging yourself,' she told him flatly.

The grin faded, showing her for the first time just how bad he really felt. His face was etched deeply with lines of pain that added years to his true age, and as he turned his head towards the light a little, she could see the fading greenish-purple remains of some startling bruises round his eyes, shot through with a truly colourful yellow.

'I was *going* out of my mind,' he corrected. 'What I need now is rest, that's all, but I'm not so suicidal that I want to go home on my own, and the last thing on God's earth I need is my mother fluttering around me like a demented hen.'

'Maybe that's exactly what you need,' Fran suggested, suppressing a smile. 'A bit of home cooking, a little motherly love, all from someone who knows you inside out—'

She was interrupted by a rude snort. 'You've never met my mother,' he said bluntly. 'She doesn't do home cooking, and she certainly doesn't know me inside out. I'm not even sure about the motherly love, but I do know she'd drive me even crazier than being in hospital. And if I don't have a nurse, she'll insist on coming to look after me, and I might just have to kill her.'

The grin surfaced again. 'You could always look on it as your moral duty as a law-abiding citizen, preventing a murder.'

The eyes twinkled in his bruised and battered face, and she crumpled. Let's face it, she thought to herself, he certainly needs help, and you aren't in a position to be fussy. Looking after him might even turn out to be fun.

'This is a live-in post, I take it?' she asked him, but her eyes were on Jackie, sitting back and watching the byplay between her newest recruit and her even newer client with avid interest.

'Jackie?' Fran prompted, wanting her input. It was her nursing agency, after all, and she was the one in charge of who went to which client and under what terms and conditions.

Jackie collected herself visibly and nodded. 'Oh, yes, it would have to be, wouldn't it, Mr Nicholson?'

He nodded agreement. 'Absolutely. The slightest loophole and my mother will be in there quicker than a sniper's bullet.'

Fran suppressed another smile. 'And the hours?'

He shrugged. 'Whatever. Minimal. However long it takes to go to the supermarket and buy some instant food and whack it in the microwave—oh, and I suppose the pins in my leg will need looking at from time to time. The rest of the time you can do what you like, so long as you're around to take me anywhere I need to go. I take it you can drive?'

'I can drive,' she confirmed.

'Well, that's fine, then. I just need a token nurse in self-defence.'

Compared to the hell on wheels of her previous job in a busy London A and E department, it sounded like a positive doddle. Her only worry was that it would be so light on the nursing that she'd get bored to death, but maybe it was exactly what she needed.

She certainly didn't feel emotionally strong enough yet to deal with anything more front line.

She glanced at Jackie, who raised an eyebrow in question. 'May be possible,' she said quietly.

Jackie smiled bracingly at both of them. 'I'm sure it will be fine.' She turned to the man. 'If you could just give us a few moments to sort out the paperwork, Fran'll be all yours,' she assured him, and then fixing Fran with a meaningful look, she led her into the office at the back. The door closed with a definite click and Jackie sagged against it, clutching her chest and sighing theatrically.

'Oh, my God, he is so *gorgeous*!' she said under her breath. 'I can't believe you know him. You are going to take this job, aren't you? You're not going to be silly?'

Fran shook her head. 'No. I'm going to see Dr Giraud at eleven, and I'm probably going to take his job—if he offers it to me. And I don't know Josh, I've only met him once.'

'Well, surely you know who he is? Good grief, he's famous—'

'Yes, they talked about him at work. I'd never heard of him,' Fran confessed. 'I gather he's got a bit of money.'

'A bit? I think the expression is "fabulously wealthy",' Jackie said with a chuckle. 'Anyway, what about the job? He needs looking after. It was a high-speed crash on the A12—something about a horse on the road. It was one of those really dark nights. Judging by the sound of it, he was very lucky to escape with his life. I'd forgotten all about it. Fran, it's the chance of a lifetime. You *have* to take the job!'

'It's a thought. At least I wouldn't be slumming it,' Fran said with a weak attempt at humour, 'and it might be quite interesting to see how the other half live. I feel a bit guilty about Xavier Giraud, though. I told him on the phone just before Josh came in that I'd go back and see him, and I was thinking about taking the job if he offered it.'

'So think about it. Do you want to work part time as a practice nurse and look after Xavier's disabled daughter in the afternoon, or do you want to work for Josh Nicholson? I know which I'd do in your situation.'

She hovered, just for a moment, haunted by the memory of Dr Giraud's rich, mellow voice with its merest suggestion of a French accent. Then she thought of the sadness in his house—the loss of his wife, the crippling injury his daughter had sustained in the accident—and wondered if she had enough caring left inside her to do the job properly. Probably not.

She shook her head. 'No. I can't do him and his daughter justice. I need a rest, Jackie. I've had enough.'

And that was it. Five minutes of paperwork, and they were off. She followed his taxi as it wove through the streets of Woodbridge, then they left the town, crossed the river and turned down a track that led through the trees. From time to time she could glimpse the river on her right, then suddenly the trees opened up to reveal his house, and her jaw dropped.

She certainly *wouldn't* be slumming it! The house was nestled in amongst the trees, a long, low curve, single storey except at the end nearest them, where the garage and a few rooms beyond it were tucked underneath, taking advantage of the natural slope. The path rose from the drive, curving round towards the front door in a long, graded sweep, and she pulled up beside the taxi and got out, awestruck.

It was *huge,* and yet oddly it blended in, cut into the landscape by the hand of a genius, and below it the river stretched out into the distance towards the sea. Slightly upstream she could see the distinctive shape of the tide mill on the opposite bank, with all the houses and shops of the old town clustered together around it and up the hill beyond.

Downstream all the little boats bobbed at their moorings, sunlight gleaming off their masts and sparkling on the wind-ruffled water, and she could almost hear the clink of halliards against the masts.

What a fabulous spot! And she was going to be living here for a while, steeped in the silence of the woodland around them. Amazing.

She pulled herself together and helped the taxi driver extract the wheelchair from the boot and ease her patient into it. Josh thanked him and paid him what seemed like an extortionate amount of money, and then suddenly they were alone.

Totally alone. Fran was suddenly aware of how isolated his house was, and how difficult it would be to get help if anything went wrong, but she suppressed the panic.

She was being silly. Nothing was going to go

wrong. He wasn't going to bleed to death, or he would have done it already. He'd be fine, and so would she. He was well on the way to recovery. All she had to do was get him into bed for a rest.

'Got the keys?' she asked him, and was met with a blank stare.

He swore softly under his breath. 'They're at the garage, with the car.'

'Is there a spare one here, hidden under a flowerpot or something?' she suggested hopefully, but he shook his head.

'Not a chance.'

'We'll have to go and get them, then,' she said pragmatically.

He eyed her car with evident disgust. 'You want me to get into that?'

Fran felt her anger flare and stamped it down. 'It may not be what you're used to—'

He sighed. 'I wasn't criticising,' he said wearily, 'I was just wondering how on earth I'm going to fold myself up inside it.'

Of course. She hadn't seen him standing up properly, but there was no mistaking the rangy length of his thighs. He was a big man, and her car was a little city car. Still, it was that or sit on the doorstep until she came back with the keys, and as she didn't know where the garage was, he might have a very long wait. She pointed this out to him, and with a quiet sigh he resigned himself to the struggle.

Josh ached. Things ached that he didn't even know he had. Her car was a nightmare, one of those cute little city cars that suited cute little city women, but it hadn't been designed with a man of his size in mind, and most particularly not one with an external fixator on his leg and umpteen other broken bones. He could kick himself for not having thought about the keys before, but all he'd cared about had been getting home and the keys hadn't really seemed a high priority then.

He shifted awkwardly in the seat so he could see her face, and he watched her as she drove. It put her off. Interesting. Her face was more interesting than he remembered, too, not classically beautiful but fine in a very English way. Her skin was a beautiful clear ivory, her hair dark and worn loose, falling in a waving, glossy curtain to well below her shoulders. He had an urge to reach out and touch it, but he thought she'd probably dump him on the road if he tried it.

She had wonderful cheekbones, and her eyes, a lovely soft grey-blue touched with lilac, spoke volumes. He wondered what had gone wrong and why a woman of her age was taking live-in jobs when she should have been at home with her husband and children or forging a dynamic career in her A and E department.

'Turn left here,' he said, and reminded himself that her reasons for working for him were none of his business. He should just be grateful that somebody suitable had been available with absolutely no notice. At least, he supposed she was suitable and hadn't been dismissed for some flagrant conduct. He imagined that she'd been vetted by the agency, but he hadn't checked. Yet another thing he'd overlooked. That wasn't like him. It must be the bang on the head.

'That's it, up ahead on the right.'

She slowed and turned onto the garage forecourt, and came to a halt. 'You stay here, I'll go and ask,' she suggested, but he shook his head.

'I want to see the car.'

'I don't think that's a very good idea,' she said firmly.

She was probably right but, nevertheless, he wanted to see it and even if he hadn't, her vetoing it was enough to get him out of the car, with or without her help.

'I don't employ you to have opinions,' he told her bluntly. 'I need a nurse, not a nanny. Get the chair.'

She opened her mouth to say something, then snapped it shut, got out of the car and slammed the door, then yanked it open again, muttering something under her breath that he couldn't quite hear. Tipping her seat forwards with a thump, she yanked his wheelchair out of the tiny space behind it and hurled the door shut again with force.

He suppressed a grim smile. So she had a temper. Even more interesting. It would make his convalescence much less tedious.

His door was yanked open and she thrust his wheelchair up against the side of the car. 'I think you're mad,' she told him with a directness that bordered on insolence, but he didn't bother to argue.

It had occurred to him while she'd been banging about in a temper that, before he struggled out of the car, it would be an idea to check that his own car was actually here on the premises, but now didn't seem the time to raise that. Anyway, George was coming over, thank goodness, a beaming smile splitting his face.

'Mr Nicholson! Good to see you, sir.'

'Hello, George. I've come to pick up some stuff from the car. I take it it's here?'

'Oh, yes, it's here. We've collected all your things together—they're in the office. I'll get one of the lads to find them for you. It's best if you stay here.'

Why were they all being so damned protective? 'I'd like to see it,' he said firmly, and he saw doubt flicker in George's eyes.

'Well, of course, if you must, it's your car after all, but I really—'

'I'd like to see it,' he repeated in a voice that brooked no argument, and with a slight shrug George gave in.

'Let me give you a hand into the chair, sir,' George said, scrubbing his oily hands on a bit of rag, and Fran moved the wheelchair back a little to give them room. Once he was settled George wheeled him through into the back of the workshop, and there, with the top missing and every panel battered almost beyond recognition, was his car.

Josh took a steadying breath and steeled himself. 'It looks a tad mangled,' he said mildly, ignoring the pounding of his heart and the nausea that had come up out of nowhere. He could see blood all over the leather seats and in the footwell, and he suddenly wondered how the hell he'd got out of it alive. He looked away.

'Um, I need the keys and the garage door remote—and any of the CDs that aren't broken. I assume it's a write-off?'

George made a smothered sound and smiled grimly. 'I think we can safely assume that, sir. The keys and the garage remote are in the office with a few other bits and pieces, but we haven't got the boot open yet and the CD player's in there. I'll drop them round to you just as soon as we've forced the lock. To be honest, sir, we weren't expecting to see you quite so soon. In fact, to be truthful, we were all pretty amazed to know you'd survived.'

Seeing the car, Josh could only agree. He nodded slightly, acknowledging George's remark, and looked up at Fran. Suddenly he'd seen enough. 'Why don't we go back to the car while George finds my things?' he suggested, hoping that for once she wouldn't challenge him.

To his amazement she didn't, just took the wheelchair from George, turned it around so he was no longer facing the mangled evidence of his close encounter with death, and pushed him back out into the sunshine. He let out a breath he hadn't known he was holding, and he felt his shoulders drop inches.

To her eternal credit she didn't say, I told you so, but merely helped him back into the car without a word and put away the wheelchair, while George handed him the keys and the remote and wished him well.

'You were quite right,' he said quietly as she drove off. 'I really didn't need to see that.'

Fran's shoulders lifted in a little shrug. 'I just knew

how it would look,' she told him. 'I've worked in A
and E for years, and I've attended lots of road traffic
accidents. It often seems quite amazing that people
survive them.'

'It all rather puts it in perspective,' he said. 'I imagine any one of the injuries might have been enough
to kill me.'

'I think it's unlikely that a broken wrist would do
it,' she teased, and he laughed, a little gusting laugh
that took more of the tension out of his shoulders.

He leant his head back against the headrest and
sighed, and she shot him a quick look, too quick for
him to be sure that it really was concern in her eyes.

'We'll soon be home,' she said gently. 'You can
have a rest and—'

'I haven't had a rest in the afternoon for years,' he
told her in disgust. 'Not since I was about three.'

'I expect there are lots of things that you've had to
do in the last two weeks that you haven't done since
you were about three, but it's no good crying over
spilt milk. And while you're sleeping,' she went on
relentlessly, 'I'll turn out the fridge, go through your
cupboards and the freezer, and then go shopping.
OK?'

What was there to say? Apparently nothing. Josh
shrugged slightly, turned his head away and stared
sightlessly out of the window. He was obviously going to have to resign himself to being fussed and
mothered by this woman, but at least she was better-
looking than his real mother, so he supposed that was
a bonus. No less opinionated, though, he realised with

a sinking feeling. They'd probably get on together like a house on fire. Oh, hell.

They turned onto the track leading to the house, and he felt every last pebble. He'd refused to take any of the painkillers they'd given him, but maybe that had been a little rash. Perhaps he'd have one when they got home. In the meantime, he gritted his teeth and said nothing.

He looked awful. The sight of the car, as she'd known it would be, had been a real shock to him. Experienced as she was, it had been a real shock to her, as well, and she still wasn't entirely sure how he'd managed to escape with his life. Fran had no idea what make it was. There hadn't been a recognisable panel on it, but she knew instinctively that it would have been almost new and hideously expensive. Not that that mattered, not compared to his life.

He was struggling now, she realised, and she wondered if he'd had any painkillers before he left the hospital. Probably not. He was stubborn enough for an entire army. Oh, well, he wouldn't die of it, he'd just feel wretched, and if that was how he wanted to play it, who was she to interfere?

The track turned into his drive, and she pulled up in front of the garage and cut the engine.

'Right,' she said, turning to him with a smile, 'all we have to do now is get you out of the car and into the house.'

Josh's answering smile was a little tight, and she thought her guess about the painkillers had probably been correct. She manoeuvred him into the wheelchair, pushed him up the grass beside the path to save having to negotiate the steps, and then once the path flattened out she pushed him quickly up to the front door and opened it with his key.

Immediately something started to beep, and he pointed across the hall towards a door. 'In there—the burglar-alarm control. Key in "5836", then "Part Set", then "No".'

She did, and the beeping stopped, to her relief. 'Right, let's get you in,' she said, and turned him round.

Hitching the wheelchair over the step was a problem, but with a little huffing and puffing she managed, and finally he was in. In fact, it wasn't until she'd retrieved his case from the car and closed the front door behind herself that she actually noticed the house, and then her jaw sagged.

There was nothing ostentatious about it, not overtly, but everything screamed quality. The solid, light oak floor, the heavy timber doors in the same pale wood as the floor, the clean, simple lines were stunning. So, too, were the original works of art on all the walls, the value of which she didn't even dare to guess at, and this was just the hall!

She shut her mouth firmly and followed his directions along the hall and into a wonderful room with a high, vaulted ceiling and a spectacular view of the river. It was a multi-purpose room, part kitchen, part breakfast area, part informal sitting room, full of rich colour and texture, and she guessed it was his favourite place in the house.

'Right, if you show me where your bedroom is I'll change your sheets and get it ready for you.'

'You don't need to change the sheets—the cleaning agency I use will have seen to it,' he told her tiredly.

'OK, in that case I'll just help you change into something more comfortable and settle you down for a while. Where is it?'

Josh waved in the direction of the door on the other side of the room, and she pushed him through it, past a glass-walled study overlooking the river, past another few doors and through the one at the end.

They must be in the room over the garage, she realised, because in the end wall there were French doors opening onto the balcony above the drive, and there was another window on the front wall with the same spectacular view as from the kitchen and study.

'Well, at least you'll have a lovely place to lie and convalesce,' she said, trying not to sound like a thunderstruck adolescent.

He grunted. 'I have no intention of lying anywhere and convalescing,' he pointed out bluntly. 'From tomorrow onwards, I have every intention of getting back to work.'

She stifled the snort of disgust, and set the brakes on the wheelchair with a decisive jab. 'We'll see,' she said crisply. 'Right, let's get you into bed.'

She leant forward, ready to tuck her right arm under his to help him up, but he just looked at her, his jaw set defiantly. 'I thought I'd already told you that I don't need a nanny,' he said, his voice deathly quiet.

She felt her eyebrows go up but was helpless to prevent it. 'So you did,' she said calmly. 'You also told me that you needed a nurse, but if you're going to be difficult and uncooperative the entire time, I'm going to have to leave. I shouldn't worry, though, because I expect your mother will be only too happy to come and look after you.'

He opened his mouth to argue, then snapped it shut, linked his arm through hers and pulled himself up out of the chair without another word. So he didn't like being threatened with his mother, she thought with a smile. How useful to know that.

Storing the little snippet for later, Fran set about undressing him, exposing yet more of the colourful bruises as well as the livid lines of his recent surgery. Under other circumstances she'd found the powerful planes and angles of his body fascinating. As it was, she ignored them, more concerned with getting him comfortably settled in bed before he keeled over. It seemed more likely with every passing second.

Josh told her where she could find soft jersey boxer shorts and a T-shirt, and she helped him into them, only too glad when he was finally lying flat on the bed and able to relax.

'Bliss,' he said with a low grunt of relief.

She eyed him thoughtfully. It would take more than simply lying down to get him truly comfortable, but how to talk him into it? Easy. Instead of asking him if he wanted a painkiller, she'd tell him it was time. She tucked a pillow in beside his leg and arranged the quilt so it didn't pull on his foot, then straightened up.

'Now, where are all the drugs they gave you when

you left the hospital?' she asked him. 'It must be time for a painkiller by now.'

For a moment he hesitated, and then he surrendered, as she'd hoped he would. 'In the case,' he muttered. 'I don't know what else there is. Antibiotics, possibly. I haven't got a damn clue.'

'That's why I'm here, so you don't have to think about it,' she said calmly. She fetched him a glass of water from the sumptuous kitchen and held it while he took the pills, then he settled back onto the pillows with a sigh.

'Thank you,' he said in a low voice.

Thank you? Good heavens. She schooled her face. 'My pleasure. Right, now I'm going to turn out the fridge so we don't get food poisoning, and if you're feeling OK I'll go to the supermarket. I've got a mobile, I'll give you the number and you can call me if you have a problem.'

She went out, leaving the door ajar, and by the time she'd emptied the fridge and made a shopping list, he was fast asleep. She wrote her mobile number on a piece of paper and tucked it under the edge of the phone on his bedside table then, taking his keys with her, she let herself out and headed back into town.

She didn't want to do a big shop, just a few basic provisions and something for tonight. After all the jostling about, she didn't really like leaving him, but all she'd found in the fridge had been a few curls of dried-up smoked salmon and a bit of cheese that had seen better days. The milk was solid in the bottle, and what few vegetables there were were well past their sell-by date. There was precious little in the cup-

boards either, and the freezer contained nothing more
than a few ready meals that left her cold.

He obviously took after his mother on the home-
cooking front, she thought dryly. Well, not any more.
Fresh vegetables, lean meat, chicken and fish and
plenty of fruit.

Her phone rang and she rummaged for it in her
bag, halfway between the carrots and the broccoli.

'Get coffee,' he said. 'Not instant—the real stuff.'

'OK. If they have it, do you want me to get some
with a Fairtrade label on it—or bird-friendly or organic or anything?'

The snort nearly split her eardrum. 'Just coffee,
Fran. Nothing clever.'

So her ultra-rich and spoilt client was a coffee addict, was he? She might have guessed. 'What sort of
beans, and what country?'

'Arabica. Don't care what country. Medium to rich
roast—and don't be long.'

'Do you miss me?' she teased.

Was that a little growl of frustration, or poor reception?

'Don't get witty—I just want the damn coffee,' he
grunted, and hung up.

Fran let the smile out, grabbed a head of broccoli
and moved on to the fruit, the chiller section and finally the coffee. It was a tiny supermarket with a
limited selection, and she couldn't be bothered to go
into town and look in a specialist shop. No Fairtrade,
no bird-friendly, not even any organic, although Josh
hadn't wanted it, but they did have Arabica in a medium roast and she decided that would have to do.

She'd sacrifice her principles on this one occasion, although she only picked up one packet. The last thing he needed was too much caffeine.

She toyed with the idea of decaff, but thought better of it. He didn't need a temper tantrum either, and caffeine enhanced the action of some painkillers, so caffeine it was.

She threw it into the trolley with all the healthy goodies she'd bought, added a packet of chocolate biscuits to satisfy his sweet tooth and headed for the checkout. Five minutes later she was on the way back to his house, and as she turned the corner of the track and pulled onto the drive, she saw him standing above her on the balcony, dressed only in his boxer shorts and T-shirt.

She got out of the car and tipped her head back, looking up at him with a mock-stern expression on her face.

'Why are you out of bed? You're standing again, and you'll catch your death. It's October.'

'I'm fine. I'm just looking at the view, breathing air that doesn't taste of disinfectant and being glad to be alive.'

Most particularly the latter, she guessed, after seeing the remains of his car. She brandished the carrier bags. 'I've got coffee,' she said with a smile, and he gave her a cock-eyed grin in return.

'Thank heavens for that. I don't suppose you got any chocolate biscuits?'

'Just a walking miracle, me,' she said cheerfully, and headed for the front door, humming softly under her breath. Maybe working for Josh Nicholson might not be so bad after all.

CHAPTER TWO

FRAN hurried up the path, let herself in through the front door and took all the bags through to the kitchen, setting them down on the breakfast bar. By the time she'd done that, Josh was there, hobbling on his damaged leg, putting far too much weight through the external fixator and wincing with every step.

'For heaven's sake, sit down, you idiot,' Fran said crossly. 'What are you trying to do, put yourself back in hospital?'

She went over to him, taking his arm and helping him down onto the soft, squashy sofa. How she would ever get him out of it she didn't know, but she'd cross that bridge when she got to it. In the meantime, he was eyeing the shopping bags like an addict waiting for his fix.

'Coffee?' he suggested hopefully.

'Patience is a virtue,' she said, probably sounding exactly like his mother, but she didn't care. She pulled all the shopping out onto the worktop, found the coffee and the coffee-maker and put them together. Within moments the kitchen was filled with the wonderful aroma of fresh coffee, and Josh was sighing with relief. While it slowly dripped through the filter, she stuffed the shopping into the fridge and cupboards, found the mugs and opened the milk, just as the front doorbell rang.

Josh groaned gently. 'Oh, hell, it's my mother,' he said under his breath.

'Shall I tell her you're in bed?' Fran offered, but he shook his head.

'Too late. She's seen me. Just let her in,' he said tiredly.

Mentally girding her loins, Fran walked calmly to the front door and opened it. A tall, elegantly dressed grey-haired woman stood there, and without a glance at Fran she swept through the door and went into the kitchen.

'Joshua, what on earth are you thinking about! You should be in hospital, you silly creature.'

She buzzed his cheek with a kiss and perched on the edge of the sofa beside him, no mean achievement considering its squashiness. Then she turned and looked at Fran, eyeing her with only slight curiosity. 'Have we met?' she asked.

Fran opened her mouth to reply, but Josh got there first.

'Mother, this is Francesca Williams, my new nurse. Fran, this is my mother, Isabel Hardy.'

Fran smiled and held out her hand, and after a moment's hesitation the woman extended her hand and took Fran's, her fingers cool and slender and beautifully manicured, quite unlike Fran's workmanlike hands. Mrs Hardy, she decided, was one of those 'ladies who lunch'.

'How nice to meet you, Mrs Hardy,' she said innocently. 'I've heard so much about you.'

'I don't doubt it,' Mrs Hardy said, eyeing her son thoughtfully. 'Where did you say you came from, my dear?'

'She didn't. The nursing agency in town—and don't patronise her, Mother. She's an intelligent woman.'

Mrs Hardy opened her mouth a fraction, but Fran just smiled and went back into the kitchen area. So he thought she was intelligent? Smart man. 'I've just put the coffee-machine on, Mrs Hardy. Can I get you a cup?'

Her elegant brow pleated. 'Are you making him coffee? Is that wise?'

'It's fine,' Fran assured her. 'A little caffeine enhances the action of painkillers, and he's had quite a difficult day, I think, what with one thing and another.'

Mrs Hardy was all ready to protest, but then Josh, obviously used to her, chipped in.

'I knew you'd worry, Mother, which is why I engaged a professional, to set your mind at rest. She's fully qualified, highly recommended, and she nags nearly as much as you do.'

Fran stifled a snort and poured the coffee. He thought she was a nag? She hadn't even started yet! 'Black or white and with or without?' she asked blithely.

Josh, as she'd remembered, took his strong, straight

and black, his mother white. Predictably, she produced a little packet of sweeteners from her bag and clicked one into her mug. Not for her the unnecessary calories of a spoonful of sugar, Fran thought with a suppressed smile.

She wondered what she was supposed to do with her own coffee. Take it below stairs to the servants' quarters? She had no idea, but the sofa seemed rather full at the moment. She propped herself up against the worktop instead, cradled her mug in her hands and blew gently onto the top of it.

'Don't nurses wear uniforms?' Mrs Hardy said after a moment, shooting Fran a suspicious look.

'Only in fantasies,' Josh said with a soft laugh, and his mother blushed furiously and swatted at his good arm.

'You're incorrigible!'

'And you love me for it.' He glanced up at Fran and smiled. 'Biscuits?' he murmured hopefully, and she put her coffee down and took out the packet, neatly slitting the end of it with a sharp knife. Now what? Hand him the packet, or put a few out onto a pretty little plate?

Plate, she thought, in view of the mother. She opened cupboards until she found the side plates, placed a few biscuits onto one and set them down on the coffee-table in front of them.

'Aren't you having one?' Josh asked her.

She shook her head. Once she started on the chocolate biscuits, she couldn't stop, so it was easier not to start. 'No, thanks,' she said, deadpan. 'I might outgrow my uniform. Anyway, I'm busy,' she added, deciding she may as well begin preparing the supper as stand there and watch them.

Something reasonably light, she thought, considering his recent surgery, but on the other hand it needed to be tasty. A nice chicken casserole, perhaps. If she could find some, she'd sling in a bit of sherry or wine or something. She poked about the cupboards, looking for some herbs or even a bouquet garni, if she was extremely lucky, but she drew a blank. Ah, well, she'd stick them on her shopping list. She hadn't expected to find them. Josh didn't really need a bouquet garni to heat a ready meal in the microwave, she thought with a little smile.

'Are you looking for something?' he asked her.

'Herbs,' she said.

'Not a chance,' he grunted. 'I told you, I don't cook.'

No, she thought, you told me your mother didn't cook. You never mentioned yourself, but it was no surprise.

'No problem,' she said lightly. 'I'll work round it for tonight.'

She would have been fine, of course, if he'd had stock cubes, but all she could find was ketchup and soy sauce. The casserole was going to be a strange one, she thought, but they'd live. While she chopped and peeled and sliced the vegetables, she kept an eye on Josh, and after a few minutes she noticed him starting to flag.

His mother was recounting some story from a bridge party, and his eyes were glazing. He glanced up and caught her eye, and his look spoke volumes. She put her knife down, washed her hands, dried them and walked over to Mrs Hardy, laying a gentle hand on her shoulder.

'Mrs Hardy, I think it's time for Josh to have a rest now, if you don't mind,' she said quietly but firmly.

Josh's mother opened her mouth to protest, but Fran just smiled, and Josh, right on cue, leant back against the sofa and sighed only slightly theatrically.

Mrs Hardy stood up, leant over him and kissed his cheek. 'You should have said, you silly boy. I didn't realise you were tired. I'll go now.'

Fran showed her to the door, closed it behind her and chuckled softly.

As she went back into the kitchen, Josh was laughing. 'Very neatly done. I owe you one for that.'

Fran picked up her coffee, went over to the sofa and perched on the other end of it.

'I meant it, really. You ought to have a rest.'

Josh shook his head. 'I really don't want to go to bed. I can't sleep at night at the best of times. The last thing I need is to sleep so much during the day that the nights are completely endless.'

'OK,' she agreed, 'but you really need to put that leg up.'

Fran stood up, took his coffee from him and, lifting

both legs at the ankle, swivelled him round. He winced a little, but then sighed with relief and dropped his head back against the arm.

'Thanks,' he murmured. 'Any chance of another coffee?'

'OK, but it's the last one. If you have any more you certainly won't sleep tonight, and I really think you need to. Which reminds me, where am I sleeping?'

'The guest room's through there,' he said, gesturing towards the hall.

Fran arched a brow. 'I don't think so. That's miles from you. How will I know if you get into difficulties in the night?'

'What kind of difficulties am I going to get into?' he asked with a chuckle. 'The mind boggles. Anyway, I thought I was going to sleep?'

'You are,' she said firmly, 'and if I have anything at all to say about it, so am I, which means I can't lie at the other end of the house straining my ears down the corridor in case you call for help. So, is there a closer room?'

He shrugged. 'Not with its own bathroom, but the room next to me has a shower opposite.'

'That'll do fine,' she said, and stood up. 'Now, you settle back and rest and I'll finish the supper.'

She went back into the kitchen and put all the ingredients together. At first he watched her, but then his eyelids started to droop and, as she'd anticipated, within moments he was asleep.

She put the casserole into the oven, and then went quietly down the corridor to the room next to his. It shared the same beautiful view, the king-size bed placed opposite the window to take full advantage of it, and she thought longingly of early mornings lying with a cup of tea, staring out across the river. What a fabulous way to start the day.

She turned down the bedspread and found the bed made up with soft, pure linen. Not for Josh's guests the polycotton sheets of normal mortals, she thought with gentle irony, and the pillows and quilt felt like goose down.

She went back through the kitchen, checking on him as she went, but he hadn't stirred and so, letting herself out of the front door, she went down to her car and retrieved her bag.

There were all sorts of things in her car, stuffed into the boot where she'd thrown them last night as she'd left London, but all she really needed was the bag. She looked down into her boot, at the carrier bags and boxes that were all she owned in the world, and with a little sigh she closed the boot lid, locked the car and went back into the house. She'd sort the rest out tomorrow.

She put the case in her room and unpacked it, and then went back to the kitchen. Josh was still sleeping, his lashes dark against his bruised cheeks, and she had a crazy urge to run her fingers over the short, dark hair. He looked vulnerable, younger with the lines of strain missing, and his mouth without the crooked grin looked soft and full and generous.

She looked down at his leg, at the pins locked to the metal bar that held the bone steady, the pins penetrating the skin and holding all the fragments in line. Judging by the number of pins, he'd been lucky not to lose it. It all looked healthy, though, she was relieved to see. The last thing he needed was a nasty infection.

Fran checked the casserole, but it was fine and didn't need her attention. Suddenly at a loose end, she wandered out into the hall and studied the paintings which until now she'd only had time to walk past. They were beautiful, full of energy, very simple and yet astonishingly lively. They were obviously by the same person, and they were signed, but she couldn't read the signature and even if she had been able to, it wouldn't have meant anything to her. She'd never studied art, she simply knew what she liked—and she liked these.

She looked at the other doors in the hall and hesitated. She didn't want to be nosy but on the other hand, it might not hurt to be familiar with the layout. At least, that was what she told herself as she turned the knob on the nearest door and entered the room.

It was the guest bedroom, of course, that he'd pointed out, more lavishly appointed than the one she'd chosen, but probably no more comfortable and without the fabulous view. She'd trade the luxury of the bathroom just for the view alone.

The next room was a library, stuffed with books, the shelves groaning. They were all real books, as well, battered old favourites as well as classics old and modern, some leather-bound, others tatty old paperbacks.

Eclectic taste, she decided, and wasn't surprised.

Then there was the dining room, and finally, after the cloakroom, the last room off the hall, furthest from the kitchen and presumably the sitting room.

She turned the knob and went in, hesitating in the doorway. She reached for the light switch, because it was growing dark now and the curtains were all closed in here, but instead of the switch there was some strange panel.

'It's electronic,' Josh said quietly behind her.

She spun round, her hand pressed her chest, guilty colour flooding her cheeks. 'You gave me such a fright!' she said with a breathless little laugh. 'How did you creep up on me?'

He gave her his crooked grin. 'Years of practice. Sorry. Here, let me.'

He hobbled towards her, wincing as he did so.

'You should be in your wheelchair,' she said in concern, 'not walking around like this. It's all right to hop from the chair to the loo, or even from the bed to the loo, but you really shouldn't be wandering around unnecessarily.'

'Are you going to nag me all the time?' he asked her mildly, and she smiled.

'Only if you make me,' she told him. 'Wait here while I get your chair.'

She hurried down to his bedroom, grabbed the chair and pushed it swiftly back into the hall. He sat down with a little grunt, and she propped his leg up on the sliding board and pushed him into the sitting room.

He reached up and tapped the keypad, and soft lights came out of nowhere and lit the room. Like the kitchen, it was vaulted, with windows on all sides to take advantage of the setting, but, unlike the warm and sunny-coloured kitchen, everything in there was very neutral and calm.

Like the hall, there was artwork everywhere, but not just paintings and drawings. In here, in addition to the pictures, there were bronzes on shelves, strangely tortured bits of twisted iron standing at one end, a plinth with a marble bust on it in the far corner—security here must be an absolute nightmare unless they were all copies, which she somehow doubted.

She said nothing, and neither did he, just watched her for her reaction and waited.

He was going to have a long wait. She felt rendered speechless, totally overawed by the astonishing investment that must have gone into this room, at the size and scale and scope of his collection, not to mention the beauty of each individual piece. Or most of them, anyway.

'Well?'

Fran shrugged, a helpless lift of her shoulders. 'What can I say? I know nothing about art, but I'm not stupid. How much do you pay a year in insurance?'

He gave a low chuckle. 'You don't want to know. Anyway, that's beside the point. What you think of them?'

'The pictures? They're lovely, all of them, and I love the bronze sculptures and the marble bust. I'm not sure about the twisted iron.'

His mouth kicked up in a smile. 'Nor am I. They're by a college student I've been sponsoring. I said I'd display them for her.' He pointed to the shelves in the alcove beside the fireplace. 'That's probably my favourite, the girl sitting on the edge of the shelf with her leg hanging down. She's a limited edition, and I was lucky to get her. She's by an artist-cum-farmer from Devon, a guy called Tom Greenshields. Unfortunately he's dead now, but he had an amazing talent—so tactile. Touch her, see what I mean.'

Fran did, running her fingers down the cool bronze, over the fine slope of the figure's shoulders and the gentle swell of her hips. She had one knee drawn up and her chin rested on it, and she was beautiful. Even her toes seemed real and solid and in proportion. Fran sighed softly under her breath. How wonderful, to have such talent, and how lucky to be in a position to collect such beautiful works of art.

'You're a very lucky man,' she murmured, and dropped her hand to her side.

'I know. I've worked hard but I've had some good breaks, although I must say the last few don't quite qualify.'

His grin was self-deprecating, and infectious. She stopped feeling jealous of him and decided to content herself with enjoying his lovely surroundings while she could. That in itself was a privilege.

'Come on, let's take you back into the kitchen and check the casserole,' she said, with a return to her usual briskness. Without waiting for Josh to comment, she turned him round and wheeled him up to the light switch, watched as he tapped it and the lights faded away, and then took him through into the kitchen.

'I hope that's going to taste as good as it smells,' Josh said, sniffing appreciatively.

'I shouldn't think there's the slightest chance,' Fran said with a laugh. 'I had to make do with only about half the ingredients. Still, it won't kill us.'

He tipped his head round and grinned up at her. 'I don't suppose there's the slightest chance of a glass of wine, is there?'

She shook her head. 'Sorry, I didn't buy any.'

His grin widened. 'If that's the only objection, I can easily overcome it. There's a cellar downstairs full of bottles of wine.'

'You probably shouldn't have more than one,' she said thoughtfully.

'Is that glass or bottle?' His eyes twinkled mischievously and she stifled a smile.

'Glass.'

'You're such a killjoy,' he said sorrowfully. 'Still, one's better than nothing. You'd better go down and choose one.'

She threw up her hands in horror. 'Not a chance! I know even less about wine than I do about art.'

'Well, I can't go down there like this, so it's you or nobody, blossom. You could always take it back and bring up another one if it's not a good choice.'

And that was that. He pointed to the door at the end of the kitchen, and she wheeled him over, set the brakes and went down the stairs to the lower floor.

'Turn right,' he instructed, 'and open that door. Now, red or white?'

She went back to the bottom of the stairs and looked up at him. 'Pass. It's got chicken, carrots, potatoes, onions, ketchup and soy sauce. You tell me.'

He muttered something that she didn't hear, and grinned. 'Try the red—on the right as you go in, about three or four along and the same up from the bottom. It should be a burgundy.'

She pulled a bottle out and peered at the dusty label.

'Côte du Rhone,' she called up to him.

'That'll do,' he replied, and she closed the door behind her and went back upstairs, handing it to him.

'OK?'

'Should be fine. Perhaps I ought to educate you while you're here,' he said with a conniving grin, but it didn't fool her.

'Nice try. Right, let's get you away from the top of the stairs before you fall down and break your neck.'

He sighed, cradling the wine on his lap as she turned him away from the top of the stairs and closed the door, then he handed it to her. 'You'd better open it,' he said. 'I don't think I'd be much use with one hand.'

She smiled cheekily. 'I don't know, what with not being able to get down the stairs to your wine cellar and not being able to take the cork out of the bottle, you're a bit stuffed really without my goodwill, aren't you?'

'Just don't shake it around,' he advised, eyeing the wine like an anxious parent. 'I know it's pretty much plonk, but it's quite decent plonk and it deserves to be treated better than lemonade.'

She rolled her eyes, but set the bottle down carefully, found the corkscrew and opened it.

'Well, you managed that all right for somebody who doesn't know anything about wine,' he said, watching her with the corkscrew.

Fran laughed. 'Just because I don't know anything about wine doesn't mean I can't open the bottle. What now?'

'Now you leave it to breathe, until we're ready to eat. Let me smell the cork.'

She put the bottle down and turned and studied him. 'Are you really that desperate?' she said with a grin.

'Cheeky. I'm just making sure it's not corked.'

'I believe you, thousands wouldn't. You look a bit better for your rest,' she said, remembering her role. 'Maybe you should go back on the sofa with your legs up and take it easy until supper's ready. Have you got a telly you can watch to help you chill?'

Josh nodded. 'There's one in that cupboard,' he said, pointing at the corner by the table. 'I'd rather listen to music, though.'

'Whatever,' she said with a shrug. 'Just so long as you rest.'

Needless to say, his choice in music was interesting. She handed him a remote control, and he aimed it at a little keypad on the wall. Moments later music flooded the room. He chose something modern and instrumental by nobody she'd ever heard of, but the beat was compelling and she found her foot tapping to the music as she prodded the casserole and prepared the vegetables.

Every now and again she glanced his way, but he was lying back on the sofa with his eyes closed, his left leg bent up and his foot tapping in time with hers, and he didn't notice her.

It gave her a chance to study him while the vegetables were cooking, and she had to admit he was a fine specimen, easily as good as she'd remembered. Broad shoulders, lean hips, well-muscled legs—at least, the left one was. The right one was suffering a bit at the moment, but no doubt it would recover. She glanced back to his face, and found him looking at her. Soft colour flooded her cheeks and she turned back to her vegetables.

'You're still alive, then?' she teased.

'Ten out of ten,' he replied, turning the music down. 'How's supper?'

'Done. Where do you want to eat?'

'Here?'

So she boned the chicken and cut it into little chunks, poured him a glass of wine and propped him up a bit, then handed him the plate on a tray. 'Heaven knows what it will be like, I make no guarantees.'

'Very wise. I never guarantee anything—that way nobody is ever disappointed.'

Fran didn't believe him for a moment. For instance, there was the art student he'd sponsored and her strange, tortured sculpture in the other room. She thought about that as she ate her supper—astonishingly palatable, considering—and thought there was a great deal more to this man than met the eye.

She sipped the wine and wondered if it was hideously expensive or if it was just Josh's company and the fact that she had found herself somewhere to live and an income for the short term at least that made everything seem better.

He swirled his glass, sniffed the wine and sipped it, and set it down with a nod of satisfaction. 'Good choice, for a self-confessed philistine,' he said with a grin. 'The casserole's good, too. If you didn't nag so much, you'd be perfect.'

High praise, indeed. She bent over her plate so that

her hair fell forward and disguised the colour in her cheeks, horribly conscious of his eyes on her.

'You need to learn to take a compliment,' he said softly.

'Lack of practice,' she told him.

'Now you're fishing.'

She didn't bother to follow that one up. There was no point. It had been so long since anybody had paid her a compliment of any sort that she couldn't remember it.

'Fran?'

'Leave it, Josh, it's not important.'

She kept her eyes fixed on her supper, and after a moment she heard the scrape of his fork against the plate again. It wasn't over, though. Even on such short acquaintance, she knew him better than that, and he would return to the subject, she'd stake her life on it.

Thank goodness it would soon be time to settle him down for the night, and she could go into that lovely room with a book from the groaning shelves in his library and just be herself. She needed the job, but more than that she needed time to recover, time to put herself back together and let herself heal.

Maybe then she'd be able to take a compliment and dare to believe it.

CHAPTER THREE

THE bed was gloriously comfortable. Fran didn't think she'd be able to sleep, but she went out like a light, even though her door was open so she could listen for Josh. In fact, she didn't wake until the first grey light of dawn teased at the edge of the curtains, and then she jumped guiltily out of bed, pulled on her dressing-gown and went into his room on tiptoe.

He was fast asleep still, his left arm flung above his head, his right arm in its cast resting across his waist. He must have been restless in the night because the pillow she'd put beside his leg to hold the quilt off it had ended up on the floor, and the quilt had slipped sideways and was pulling on his foot, turning it outwards.

Rats. She should have checked him earlier, because she didn't want the pulling of the quilt to twist his femur before it had healed. Creeping quietly across the room, she tucked the pillow in beside his leg again and eased the quilt up to relieve the pressure.

He stirred, murmuring something unintelligible, and then his lids fluttered open and he looked at her with sleep-glazed eyes.

'Morning,' she said softly. 'I didn't mean to wake you, but the quilt was pulling on your foot.'

'Thanks,' he said, his voice gruff. 'It keeps slipping. I must have kicked the pillow out of the way. How did you sleep?'

She gave a sheepish smile. 'Rather too well. I meant to keep an eye on you, but I just didn't wake up. How about you?'

He shrugged. 'Not too bad. Better than usual. There's nothing quite like being in your own bed in your own home.'

Fran didn't know about that. It seemed a long time since she'd had her own bed. She'd been living in rented flats and hospital accommodation for the last nine years, and she wasn't sure if she'd had a place in all that time that she would have called home. She certainly didn't have one now, that was for sure, not since she'd walked out the night before last.

She made a noncommittal noise, twitched the quilt again and headed for the door. 'Well, if you're all right, I may as well go back to bed.'

'Will you sleep?'

His voice checked her, and she paused in the doorway. 'Probably not, but I can read while you sleep.'

'I won't sleep again, but I could murder a cup of tea.' His grin, as usual, totally undermined any resistance she might have had to his charm, but she didn't mind. Tea seemed like a good idea.

'And a painkiller?' she suggested.

Josh hesitated for a moment, so she went on, 'You're going to want to get up and go to the bathroom and wash, and you'll probably want to change, so a boost of pain relief now might be quite sensible.'

He nodded. 'You're absolutely right—as usual. Don't you find it rather boring, being right all the time?'

If it hadn't been for the teasing smile lurking in his eyes, she might have thought he was being critical. As it was, she gave him an answering smile of her own and shook her head. 'Oh, no, I never find it boring, being right. Just as well, really. I'd be bored all the time!'

Josh's chuckle followed her up the corridor to the kitchen, staying with her while she made the tea.

She took it with a glass of water and his painkillers down to his bedroom on a tray, propped him up in bed against a pile of pillows and set the tray down in front of him, taking her mug of tea and heading for the door.

'Where are you going?' he asked.

She shrugged. 'Back to my room?'

'Stay here,' he said, in a voice somewhere between a command and an entreaty. 'Keep me company. It's been a very long, boring night.'

It wasn't strictly speaking part of her job to entertain him at six o'clock in the morning, but if it affected his mental well-being, then she supposed in a way it was.

She looked around his room for somewhere to sit, and her eyes landed on a big, squashy chair by the window. She opened the curtains beside it to reveal the beautiful view. A pale, ghostly mist was curling off the river and hiding the town from sight, only the occasional church spire sticking up out of the shroud to give away the secret. Above it the sky was a pale azure blue, and she realised it was going to be a glorious day once the sun rose.

Some people got all the tough breaks, she thought with an inward smile, deciding that this was one part of her job she was more than happy to do. There was something ethereal about the mist on the water, and she curled up in the chair with her feet under her bottom, the mug cradled in her cupped hands, and gazed out over it, letting it soak into her soul.

'This is such a wonderful spot. How on earth did you get planning permission to build here?' she asked him after a moment.

'I didn't. Somebody else had started it and run out of money, and he owed me a whole lot more, so I took it off him in settlement of the debt. It was the best day's work I ever did. And as to how he got planning permission, well, rumour has it that money changed hands, but I don't know how much truth there is in that. Probably none. There was originally something here, and the planners are always more lenient under those circumstances. Anyway, permission had been granted, and so I had it finished with a few modifications here and there, and I've been here ever since. Oddly enough, you can hardly see it from the other side of the river.'

And she imagined that suited him. For all his enormous wealth, he didn't seem in the least bit ostentatious—well, if you discounted the works of art, of course.

'I've been thinking,' she said. 'You know those strange tortured creatures in the sitting room?'

He chuckled. 'You mean Annie's sculptures?'

'Wouldn't she do better if they were in a gallery?'

'Absolutely, of course she would, but there aren't very many galleries that will take such off-the-wall pieces, especially round here. Most of them aren't interested in total unknowns, although as far as I'm concerned, Annie's got more art in her little finger than the average Turner Prize-winner has in their entire body. In fact, because of that I'm doing something about it, or I should say I was until I had my accident. I've bought an old warehouse on the riverside and it's in the process of being converted to a gallery at the moment. I should really be down there overseeing it now.'

Fran's eyebrows arched. 'At six o'clock in the morning?'

Josh laughed softly. 'Well, maybe not just yet. Maybe when I've had a shower and some breakfast—'

'Shower?'

'You've got a problem with that?' he grunted, eyeing her warily.

'No, but your plaster cast might have. I'll have to find a bin bag or something and tape it over it. Have you got a seat in the shower?'

He shook his head. 'No, but you'll find a plastic garden chair if you go down to the garage. You could stick that in there, if you must.'

'I must. You were standing on that thing far too much yesterday, and if you aren't careful, you're going to rotate your leg on that femur pin and end up with your foot sticking out sideways for the rest of your life.'

He gave a resigned sigh. 'Yes, Nursy,' he chanted, and she suppressed a smile.

'That's better,' she said, deadpan. 'More tea?'

Josh lay in bed, listening to the sounds of Fran going down to the garage beneath to find a chair. She was proving very easy to have around but, nevertheless, he felt helpless and ineffectual, and that was something he just wasn't used to.

He was always on the go, busy, dynamic—all this endless inactivity was going to get right on his nerves, and there were weeks more of it lined up ahead of him. Even the thought of it was enough to drive him crazy.

Fran came back into the room, victoriously carrying a plastic garden chair in her arms. 'I think it'll need a bit of a shower itself before you sit on it,' she said. 'I might have to go in there with it and give it a good scrub down.'

Josh had a sudden and shockingly vivid image of Fran naked, bending over in his shower and scrubbing away at the chair, and he felt his body stir. Well, that answered that question at least. Everything still worked.

He closed his eyes and groaned softly under his breath. Just so long as she didn't insist on accompanying him into the shower in order to scrub him as well, he'd be fine, but he had a horrible, sinking feeling she'd be in there with a bar of soap and a flannel, scrubbing every nook and cranny.

Well, he'd just refuse to let her, and she could draw her own conclusions.

'I'll just get a towel from my bathroom, and my wash bag, if that's OK? I may as well do me and the chair at the same time.'

'Fine,' he managed between gritted teeth. He wouldn't think about it. He just wouldn't.

He did. He heard the sound of the water, the gentle bump as the shower door slid shut, Fran's little squeal as she turned the water on and was sprayed from all directions by the power-shower jets. Whoops. He'd forgotten to tell her about that. He gave a grim smile and tried not to think about her, but it was impossible. He could hear the water splashing on her, picture her in his mind's eye, and his body was having a great time.

Damn. He sat up a little more, accidentally pushing down on his right hand to hoist himself up the bed, and pain shot up his arm. Good. Perhaps that would settle him down a little.

Josh lay back against the pillows with a groan of frustration and closed his eyes. Reaching out for the

remote control, he turned on the hi-fi system, select-
ing a CD with enough life and volume to drown out
the sound of her showering, and forced himself to
concentrate on the plans for the gallery.

He needed to think about it—needed to think about
anything, really, that would distract him at the moment, because any minute now she was going to come
out of the bathroom and try and get him out of bed,
and he was going to be acutely embarrassed!

So think about the gallery, Nicholson, he told himself firmly. Think about the gallery...

Josh's shower was amazing. In fact, the entire bathroom was amazing. It was tiled to the ceiling with
huge marble tiles, and the fittings were fabulous. The
shower cubicle itself was big enough to hold a party
in, and the water came at you from all sides as well
as from above.

It was wonderful—invigorating and utterly self-
indulgent—and she stayed in there far too long. Still,
at least the chair was clean!

Fran stepped out of the shower cubicle, wrapped
herself in the huge bath sheet she had found in the
shower room opposite her bedroom and looked
around.

The bath was vast, set in an alcove with lights
above it, and it was easily big enough for two. It was
the sort of stuff, she thought, that fantasies were made
of, and she found herself picturing Josh in here, not

mangled up as he was at the moment, but fit and well and full of energy.

She could imagine him in the shower, singing in a great deep, bass voice as he lathered himself, or in the bath, up to his neck in bubbles, sitting opposite some society blonde and sipping champagne.

She felt a stab of something that felt curiously like jealousy, and it stopped her in her tracks.

What on earth was she thinking about? He was a patient! She'd never done this before in her life. With a ragged sigh, she leant back against the tiled wall and stared out of the skylight. She must be crazy. He was a multimillionaire, a good-looking man in his prime, and she was just a boring little nurse employed by him to keep his mother out of his hair. He could have no possible interest in her, and she'd do well to remember that!

Shrugging away from the wall, she scrubbed herself roughly dry with the towel, pulled on her clean clothes and scooped up her night things, winding her hair up into the soggy towel. The sooner she got him through the shower, dressed and out of the house, the better it would be for her sanity.

Fran opened the door and went back into his bedroom, to find him lying there with his eyes closed, listening to some obscure piece of music with evident concentration.

'Your turn next,' she said brightly, and whisked into her bedroom, closing the door behind her with a sigh of relief. She hung up the towel in the shower-room opposite, folded her nightdress and dressing-gown and dragged a comb though the tangled rats' tails of her hair. Once order was restored to it, she scraped it back into a ponytail and went back into Josh's room armed with a bin bag and some sticky tape that she'd found in a drawer in the kitchen.

'If you tell me what you'd like to wear, I can get it out for you and have it ready for you to put on after your shower.'

He pressed a button on the remote and the room was plunged into silence.

'Jeans,' he said tersely. 'I've got some with a fairly loose cut. They'll be in the third drawer down in the dressing-room, on the left-hand side.'

She went in there and retrieved clean underwear, several pairs of jeans and a comfortable blue chambray shirt. She took the jeans over to him to choose the right ones, and he pulled a pair out of the pile and gave them to her.

'These,' he said.

'Shirt OK?' she asked him.

Josh nodded, and she dropped them onto the foot of the bed with the other things, put the rejected jeans back in the drawer and shut it with a little bang.

How about 'please' and 'thank you'? she thought crossly. Something had obviously put him in a foul mood. She took a deep breath and went back to him. 'Right, we need to cover this arm up in something waterproof,' she said, and taped him in. Finally satisfied that it was waterproof enough to withstand the force of that astonishing shower, she stood back.

'All ready?'

He gave a curt nod, quite unlike the person he'd been up till now, and she wondered if he was in pain or if something had happened while she'd been in the shower. A phone call from his mother?

Fran helped him into the bathroom, and then he turned to her, not quite meeting her eyes. 'I can manage now, thank you, if you could just hang around in case I get into trouble?'

She blinked. 'Fine,' she said, a little surprised. 'I'll make your bed, and see if I can find a better way of anchoring that pillow. Just shout if you need me.'

Did she imagine it, or was there a faint brush of colour on the back of his neck as he turned away?

Josh Nicholson, coy? What a novel thought.

She went out, closing the door behind her with a soft click, and while she tidied his bed she kept an ear open in case he got into difficulty. What if he slipped on the wet tiles and fell? She'd never forgive herself. A friend she'd trained with had broken her femur in a car accident, and had slipped and landed on her knee only four weeks later, bending the pin. Her leg was never straight again.

She couldn't allow that to happen to Josh while he was in her care. Modest or not, she owed it to him to look after him better than that, and he had nothing she hadn't seen before thousands of times, even if it wasn't usually quite so decoratively packaged.

She tapped on the door and stuck her head around it, and found him sitting in the chair in the shower cubicle, his head tipped back while the full force of the water blasted down on him.

He was totally unaware of her presence, and it was only when she tapped on the glass that he noticed her. He started slightly, reached up, turned off the water and opened the door a fraction.

'I didn't call.'

'I know. I just didn't want you to slip when you got out. Are you finished?'

Josh sighed and nodded briefly, and she took the towel off the heated towel rail, slid the door wide open and held the towel out to him at chest height. He stood, taking it from her and wrapping it firmly round his waist, and she tucked it in for him and helped him out down the step.

'Hang on,' she said. Picking the chair up, she shook it to remove the worst of the water and set it down behind him. 'Sit on that,' she instructed. 'I'll get another towel and dry your legs.'

Fran was very gentle with his lower leg, blotting it carefully dry around the entry site of the pins. The surgeon had done a good job, she thought, because it had obviously been a nasty break. Then she dried between his toes, rubbed the towel briskly over the other leg and foot and threw it at him. 'Here, you can dry the rest.'

He took the towel in his left hand and rubbed it over his head, wincing slightly from time to time. Of course, he'd had a burr hole to remove a clot. She'd forgotten that. Heavens, the poor man must hurt from end to end, quite literally. No wonder he was a little bit grumpy.

Without a word she took the towel from him and finished the job, glad to see that the bin bag had worked and that his cast was still dry.

There was a tiny scar where she'd stitched his cut three weeks ago. She remembered how she'd teased him about losing his looks, never dreaming he'd so nearly lose his life just days later.

A dribble of water ran down the side of his face, and she blotted it gently away from the dark stubble of his jaw.

'Better now?' she asked, her voice softened by guilt because she'd been cross with him for being bad-tempered when he'd just been in pain.

Josh nodded again, just a slight movement of his head, and gave her a crooked little smile. 'Much, thanks. All I need now is my clothes on and some breakfast, and I might feel almost human again.'

Pity, Fran thought. He was looking much too human to her and far too little like a patient at the moment. Not that her patients weren't human, but they weren't usually quite that good at it, she thought with a wry little smile.

'Clothes and breakfast coming up,' she said cheerfully. Fetching Josh's wheelchair, she helped him into it and pushed him back into his bedroom.

*   *   *

'So this is your gallery?' Fran said, gazing around her at the open interior of the old brick-built warehouse on the quay.

'One day.' Josh scanned the area, curious to see what had been done in his absence over the last two weeks. There had been some progress, he supposed, but probably not as much as he'd hoped. 'It'll be kept open,' he told her, 'with dividers to break up the space and hang things on. That'll make it more flexible. It's due to open before Christmas, but I'm not sure if it'll happen.'

'It's wonderful. Are you going to keep all the bits of machinery? Some of them are quite interesting.'

'We hope to. Part of the idea is to have it as a sort of museum, with a coffee-shop-cum-tearoom and maybe a small bookshop or card shop or something, because we won't charge for entry. We don't want to detract from the tide mill, though. Hopefully, it'll run alongside and they'll bring custom to each other. It's only a reasonably short walk along the quay and, oddly enough, there's precious little to do on the riverside. Anyway, that's OK, it's all going all right. Now I need to go and buy another car, because I don't think I can bear being driven around in that tiny little machine of yours very much longer and, besides, I don't see why we should use your car to run me around.'

'I wouldn't mind at all if you didn't keep insulting it,' Fran said with a slightly twisted grin.

He shook his head. 'I'm sorry, and I know it was

ideal for what you had it for, but after the XK8 it just seems a wee bit tiny. And to be honest,' he admitted, 'I feel just a bit vulnerable in it. I'd rather have a lot more metal around me.'

They went to Ipswich, to the Jaguar garage where he'd bought the XK8, and Fran looked at him in horror.

'I hope you're not expecting me to drive you around in a Jag?' she exclaimed.

'Why not? They're good cars, and dead easy to drive. I don't see the problem.'

'Oh, don't you?' She pulled up on the forecourt, cut the engine and folded her arms. 'I hate big cars. I know you're feeling nervous, and I can understand that, but it's nothing to how I'll feel if I have to drive around in thousands of pounds' worth of car, trying not to ricochet off everything I encounter.'

Josh sighed. 'So, what would you drive around in?' he asked her, totally puzzled by her attitude.

She shrugged. 'I don't know—a Ford? A Vauxhall? Something—you know, normal.'

'You need to live a little,' he said with a slight smile. 'Come on, we'll go in and find somebody to show you a few things and take you out in them. Maybe you'll change your mind then.'

'And maybe pigs will fly,' she muttered under her breath.

'Ah, come on, for heaven's sake!' he said impatiently. 'We're only talking about a damn car! What does it matter if you crash it?'

'What does it matter? *What does it matter!* You've just nearly *killed* yourself crashing your car—have you forgotten? Have you forgotten what it looked like after they cut you out of it? What are you talking about?'

He just sighed and leant back against the headrest. 'Of course I haven't forgotten what it looked like. Of course I haven't forgotten my crash, but you're talking about not being able to judge where the corners of the car are, not avoiding a horse in the dark at seventy miles an hour! If I'd been driving anything else, I probably would have been killed, so don't give me that rubbish. And there's no way that I'm going to be driven round in this tin can any longer than I absolutely have to, so get used to it!'

For a moment, she didn't move, and then she turned on him, her eyes spitting violet sparks.

'That is *it*!' she exploded. 'I've known you less than twenty-four hours, and you're slagging off my car *again*! Just where do you think you get off? If you don't like my car, perhaps you could get your mother to drive you around or hire a taxi. But one thing's for sure, I'm not doing it any more. You are the most ungrateful, evil-tempered—'

'Hey, come on, that's not fair!'

'Nor is slagging off my car, but you seem to think that's fine!'

Josh reached out a hand and touched Fran's shoulder, but she shrugged it off roughly and turned away. Not, however, before he saw the sparkle of tears in her lovely grey-blue eyes. Oh, hell, it was going to take some fancy footwork to get him out of this one.

'Fran, I'm sorry,' he said heavily. 'I didn't mean it to come out like that.'

'Maybe not, but it was what you meant. Well, I meant it, too. I'm not going to drive you around any more if you go on like this.'

He gave a mental sigh of relief. For a moment, he'd thought she hadn't meant to finish that sentence and was going to turn him out onto the forecourt and leave him there.

'How about something different?' he asked, trying again.

'How about something cheaper? How about something that doesn't cost the same amount as the average three-bedroom terraced house?'

'OK. How about…a used four-wheel-drive?'

She shot him a suspicious look. 'What, one of those big, high things that they use for pulling horse boxes?'

He suppressed his grin. 'I thought most people just had them to pick up the kids from school,' he said mildly. 'You couldn't do one of those much harm, and you get a good view out of them. You can see where everything is for miles around, they're a piece of cake to drive, and it wouldn't hurt me to have one for when the weather gets bad. The track can be pretty unfriendly after heavy rain or snow.'

She hesitated for a moment, then shrugged. 'OK,' she said. 'Where to?'

*   *   *

'It's new!'

'No, it's not, it's used.'

'It's one year old! That doesn't count as used. That's just barely run in. I thought you meant something ancient?'

'It might as well be reliable,' he said reasonably, and gave her what he hoped was a winning smile. It seemed to work because, with a reluctant grin, she opened her car door, got out and retrieved his wheelchair from behind the seat. She didn't even slam the door, he thought with relief, so maybe she wouldn't poison him when they got home. His door opened and she locked the wheels on the wheelchair and helped him into it.

'OK, I'll try it,' she agreed, 'but if it scares me to death, please, don't buy it and expect me to drive you round in it.'

'Of course not,' he said soothingly, his fingers crossed under the cover of his cast. 'Let's just go and talk to the salesman.'

Amazingly, she liked it. Not only did she like it, she actually seemed to enjoy driving it. Thank heavens for that, he thought. He just hoped she didn't catch sight of the price ticket, because the one-year-old diesel Range Rover with its automatic gearbox, leather seats, air-conditioning, CD player, air suspension and other assorted gadgets was every bit as expensive as the Jag he'd intended to get.

Ah, well, at least he'd get a good view as he was

driven round the countryside, and it was easy for him to get in and out of, oddly enough, despite being high.

'OK?' he asked her.

Fran turned to him, her eyes sparkling. 'Oh, yes, it's great. I love it!'

He turned his head and looked at the salesman in the seat behind her. 'Done,' he said with a smile. And that was that. Half an hour later, he'd arranged to have it delivered later in the morning, and they were on their way home, for what he sincerely hoped would be his last trip in her little car.

'I have to say,' she announced as she hoiked his wheelchair out from behind her seat, 'it'll be easier to get the wheelchair in and out of.'

'This would be easier if you put the wheelchair in the boot,' he pointed out to her.

'The trouble is, my boot's full,' she explained. 'I moved out of my flat the night before last, and everything is in there.'

Josh felt his eyebrow shoot up. 'Everything?'

'We don't all have a valuable art collection,' she retorted, slamming the door vigorously.

It seemed their truce was at an end.

CHAPTER FOUR

THE atmosphere, after that, was strained in the extreme.

Fran took Josh into the house, suggested that he have a rest and then took herself off into the garden on the pretext of bringing in some things from the car.

Instead, she walked down the path, leant against the back of her car and stared out over the river. The awful emptiness of her life suddenly seemed overwhelming. Who am I? she thought. What have I done? I'm twenty-six, nearly twenty-seven, and everything I own in the world fits in the boot of my very small car. I don't have a home any more, I don't have a job any more with any future in it, I've got nothing.

Tears prickled at the back of her eyes, and she brushed them angrily away. Self-pity wouldn't get her anywhere, she realised, and, shrugging away from the car, she walked down towards the river. The sun was glorious now, surprisingly warm for the time of year, and she let it soak into her and ease away the dull ache inside.

How long she stood there she didn't know, but when she turned to walk back to the house she saw

Josh standing on the balcony outside his bedroom window, watching her.

'I'm just enjoying the gorgeous day,' she called with artificial cheer.

'So I see,' he replied. 'Here, the remote control for the garage doors. You could put your car away while you're there. I'd rather not have it on the drive, I don't like to advertise when I'm in or out. Keep them guessing.'

He tossed the little gadget down to her, and she caught it, staring at it suspiciously. She hated gadgets. Oh, well.

She looked up to ask him how it worked but he'd turned away already and was heading back inside, limping heavily, and she shook her head in despair. She wished he wouldn't walk on it so much but, short of breaking his other leg, there didn't seem to be a way to stop him.

Fran studied the remote control. There was a set of two buttons on each side, a red one above, a green one below. She pressed the green one on the left and the left-hand door whirred slowly into life, rising up and lifting out of the way.

So far so good. She drove her car in, abandoned it in the middle of the vast space and got out. As an afterthought she opened the boot and removed one or two things to act as her alibi, then after a couple of shots she persuaded the remote to close the door and went through the door and along the corridor towards the stairs from the kitchen.

By the time she arrived Josh was in there, ensconced on the sofa with his legs up and a distinct grey tinge to his skin. Guilt tugged at her, and with a quick glance at her watch she hurried to get him a painkiller and a glass of water. She should have been here to help him, she thought, and then reminded herself that if he hadn't been so sarcastic and nasty about her few possessions, she would have been.

And anyway, it was his fault he was in so much pain. He shouldn't try to do so much so soon, the stubborn idiot.

She handed him the pill and the glass, expecting a protest, but for once he took it without a word, handing back the empty glass a moment later. She avoided his eyes, though, still too cross and tangled up inside to deal with him yet.

'Any chance of a coffee before lunch?'

She nodded, put the machine on and took her things through to her bedroom, dumping them on the floor of the built-in wardrobe. She didn't need anything out of the bags anyway. It had only been an excuse to escape for a minute.

Fran sat down on the bed and stared blindly out across the river. She seemed to be doing rather a lot of that at the moment. She gave a weary sigh. The peace and tranquillity of this setting and the very limited amount that she could do for Josh left her with little to occupy her mind, and that was bad news.

She'd thought she'd needed a rest, but she was so used to running flat out, living in chaos and bustle and noise, that to be buried in the depths of the quiet Suffolk countryside was rather too much of a contrast, and her mind kept going back over the last few weeks, over and over again.

Oh, well, she'd just have to throw herself into the housekeeping role a bit more thoroughly, she thought. More cooking now, and then, while Josh was resting this afternoon, more shopping, perhaps. Heavens, she could hardly wait.

She went back into the kitchen, poured him a cup of coffee and inspected the contents of the fridge unenthusiastically.

'What are you looking for?' he asked.

'Inspiration,' she replied under her breath, then pulled her head out of the fridge and looked at him over the door. 'What do you fancy for lunch?'

'Anything. So long as I don't have to make it, I'm easy. Sandwiches?'

She shook her head. 'Not till I go and get some ingredients. Cheese on toast?'

'Fine.'

Fran busied herself, trying not to notice him at the other end of the kitchen, but it was difficult to ignore him when he was sitting there watching her every move over the top of his coffee-cup.

By the time it was done she was ready to scream, but she stifled the urge and dished up, carrying the two plates over to the sofa and sitting down at the other end, careful to avoid his legs.

'Thanks,' he said quietly, and took the plate from

her without a murmur. They ate in silence, then with a sigh Josh put his plate down and looked at her.

'Fran?'

She put the last piece of cheese on toast down on the plate again and turned to face him. 'What?' she said warily.

He scrubbed his left hand over the short-cropped hair and gave a ragged sigh. 'Look, I'm sorry,' he said gruffly. 'I've been a complete pig today, haven't I? I was rude about your car when what I really should have been doing was thanking you for taking me round in it, and then I tried to bully you into driving a car that you didn't feel comfortable with. Then for some reason you took my comment about the things in your car quite the wrong way, I don't know why, but it clearly upset you.'

He sighed again. 'Whatever, I'm sorry. I'm just sore and grumpy and frustrated, and you were there in the firing line.' His mouth kicked up on one side in a rueful smile. 'Forgive me?'

How could she not, when he was only half to blame? The car *was* small and she did have ridiculously few possessions, and if she hadn't been so used to driving a tiny car for such a long time, she probably would have loved to have a Jaguar. If anything, the Range Rover that she'd taken to like a duck to water was even bigger.

'There's nothing to forgive,' she told him. 'You were crabby, I was hypersensitive. I should say we're probably even.'

Josh's smile widened, taking in his eyes. 'You're too generous,' he murmured, 'but since I seem to be winning here, any chance of another coffee?'

'You're such a cupboard lover,' she said with a mock frown, getting up and taking his cup over to the coffee-machine. However, before she could fill it, she heard a car drive up outside. 'That might be your Range Rover, talking of cars,' she told him, and went quickly down the corridor and through his bedroom to look down onto the drive.

She hurried back. 'It is. Shall I go out and make sure everything's OK and sign for it?'

He nodded, and she hurried down the path, curiously excited. It was like taking delivery of a new toy, and it didn't seem to matter that it wasn't hers. She was handed a wad of papers, two sets of keys and a delivery note to sign, then the man from the garage waved her goodbye, got into the other vehicle that was waiting and drove off. She went back up the path and inside to Josh, and dropped the keys and the paperwork on his lap with a flourish.

'You are now the proud owner of a very smart car,' she said with a big grin.

He smiled back, enjoying her enthusiasm, although it must have been the umpteenth time that he'd done it so it was hardly virgin territory for him.

Still, he seemed quite pleased. He tossed the keys up in the air and caught them with his left hand. 'Fancy taking it for a run?'

She shrugged. 'Sure. Where to? Anywhere special?'

'I ought to go back to the gallery,' he told her. 'I need to see the builder really, and he wasn't there this morning. If he's not there this afternoon, I shall want to know why. And if he is there, you could go and do that shopping you keep talking about—which reminds me, what do I owe you from yesterday? I was so busy hurting I didn't even think about it.'

'I'm not sure. I've stuck the receipt in the cutlery drawer. I'll add it onto today's, if you like, and you can give me a cheque, or you can give me cash, or whatever.'

He pulled his wallet out of his back pocket and fished around, then handed her a cashpoint card and told her the pin number.

She sat down abruptly on the coffee-table. 'Are you crazy? You don't know me from Adam,' she told him bluntly. 'Or do you have so much money that it just doesn't matter?'

He gave a soft huff of laughter. 'A bit of both. I trust you. I'm a pretty good judge of character usually, and even if you did decide to abscond, there's a two-hundred-pound daily limit on that card anyway. I reckon you're worth the risk.'

She shook her head slowly. 'You're very trusting.'

'No. No, I'm not, but I do believe in my instincts, and I know you're not a thief.'

'I might be desperate,' she told him.

Josh shook his head. 'No. I don't think so—well,

not in that way, although I might be wrong. It's odd. You're living here in my house, with access to my wallet, my papers, my art collection—there are no end of ways in which you could take advantage, and yet I know next to nothing about you. I know you used to live in London and work in a busy A and E department, and I know the contents of your flat are in the boot of your car, but apart from that I know nothing. I don't know why you're here, what you're running away from—nothing.'

'I'm not running,' she corrected him. 'I walked away. It was quite cold-blooded and deliberate. I left my job because I couldn't do it any more, and I left my flat because I found my flatmate in bed with the man I thought I was going out with.'

His eyes scanned her face for a moment, then he closed them and shook his head gently. 'Hell, I'm sorry. That must have hurt.'

'Surprisingly little. I would have credited him with better taste, but I didn't really care, not about him, and I shouldn't really have expected more of her. She wasn't what you could call fastidious about anything. Believe me, living in a clean, tidy house again is wonderful.'

He said nothing for a moment, just watched her, then he sat up and shifted his legs carefully to the ground. 'Let's go out in the car,' he said. 'I could do with a breath of fresh air, and I reckon you could, too. To hell with the gallery and the shopping. Let's go to Aldeburgh and go for a walk along the front.'

Fran looked at him and gave a gentle, mocking laugh. 'Excuse me? A walk?'

He grinned a little off kilter. 'Well, you can walk and I can ride—or we can just park on the front and look at it with the windows open and pretend we're getting exercise.'

'That sounds more like it,' she said with a laugh, and stood up. 'Stay there, I'll fetch your chair. I think it's time I started earning my keep. Just don't move a muscle.'

'While I think about it,' he told her, 'there's a letter for my GP from the hospital telling them I'm a rebel. I suppose we ought to drop it in, just in case.'

'We should. I didn't even think about it. They should have had it yesterday. Where is it?'

'In my case, in the little side pocket.'

She went to find it, tucked it in her handbag and then went to sort him out. Five minutes later they were ready to leave, and she set the alarm and took him down to the new car.

So much for his rest, she thought as she helped him into it, but he'd been lying on the sofa for quite a while, and she didn't intend to be out for long, an hour at the most.

And then Josh was definitely going to bed!

Apart from nearly taking out the side of the car on the hedge a couple of times because of the unaccustomed width, Fran managed fine, Josh thought with an inward sigh of relief, and he settled back to enjoy the view.

'It seems odd, being all the way up here,' he said to her, peering into the gardens they passed.

'It's wonderful. I've never seen the attraction before, really, but it's so easy to drive because you can see all the corners, and you can be amazingly beaky— I mean, look in there! What a fabulous garden, but you'd never know from this side if you couldn't see over.'

He looked, and winced as she strayed a little close to the hedge again and he heard the death knell of his paintwork for the third time. 'Do you think we could save the off-roading for later?' he asked dryly, earning himself a dirty look.

'So-orry,' she said, sounding peeved, but he just shrugged. It was his car, and if she was going to drive it, she was going to have to put up with his comments.

After that she strayed, if anything, too far the other way, but Josh kept his mouth shut and gave her time. She'd soon get the measure of it, he was sure, and he didn't want to be dumped in Aldeburgh—or, worse still, the middle of the forest!

He'd phoned his insurance brokers and put Fran on the insurance while she'd been out in the garden taking umbrage, and he'd realised he didn't know her date of birth, her home address, anything. To be on the safe side he'd covered the car for anyone over twenty-five, then changed it to twenty-one because he wasn't even sure about that.

'How old are you?' he asked suddenly, and she glared at him.

'Are you implying that I'm being childish?'

'Actually, no, but since you mention it...'

'I just don't like being criticised.'

'None of us do. Why I was asking was because I just had to give the insurance company some details about you, and I realised I had no idea.'

'Oh.' She subsided visibly. 'I'm twenty-seven—well, I will be next week, anyway.'

'Does that make you a Scorpio?'

'Yes. What are you?' she asked suspiciously.

'Cancer.'

'Oh, hell. Two water signs. We're bound to fight and take the hump all the time.'

'Absolutely—so, when I've said something and you've taken it the wrong way, just remember that it might be nothing more than that and it isn't necessarily a criticism.'

Josh shot her a smile, and after a moment she smiled back, a wry, twisted little smile that did something funny to his heart. He sat back, propping himself against the window, and watched her and the view all the way to Aldeburgh.

They had a cup of tea in a hotel overlooking the sea, because it was too cold to sit outside in the wind for long, and then she drove him back—faultlessly. He was glad about that, because he was starting to hurt again, and his leg was throbbing from hanging down.

'Right, I think you need a rest,' she said as she manoeuvred the wheelchair over the step, and he was only too ready to agree. He even let her undress him, because he couldn't be bothered to argue, and within minutes he was settled down between the soft, cool covers and the painkiller she'd just given him was beginning to take effect.

'Thank you,' he said softly as she closed the curtains and headed for the door.

She paused. 'My pleasure. That's why I'm here, remember? To look after you? I'm only doing my job.'

Her temporary job, he thought, and at the moment she had no home.

'No fixed abode'—wasn't that what the police referred to it as? He tried to imagine what it must be like to have no roots, no home, no place to call your own. No retreat.

Hideous. He couldn't imagine anything more terrifying. Was Fran terrified? Scared of being homeless and unemployed? Why couldn't she do her job any longer? Not because she'd done anything wrong, he'd stake his life on it. When she'd told him, she'd sounded sad, not evasive or defensive.

Had it just become too much? He'd heard of that happening to people who worked on the front line of the emergency services. Had it happened to Fran?

Whatever, he was glad she was here, for all her prickliness and the fine network of scratches down the near side of his new car. He felt safe, knowing she was around.

Safe? What an odd word to come up with. He'd never felt unsafe in his life, he thought, drifting gradually off, but it was a lovely thought. Safe...

His lids drooped shut, and he was gone.

Fran curled up in the corner of the kitchen sofa with a book she'd found in the library and stared out over the river. It was still only mid-afternoon, and she had shopping to do, and that doctor's letter to drop in at the surgery.

She didn't know which surgery it was, she hadn't looked at the envelope, but no doubt she'd be able to find it. It worried her that they hadn't had the letter yet, but if anything happened to Josh she'd get him whisked straight back into hospital, so to a certain extent it was irrelevant whether or not the GP knew about his injuries.

Still, she didn't really want to leave him while he was asleep, although realistically it was the best time, she knew, because at least he wouldn't overdo it. She gnawed her lip thoughtfully, then sighed. No, she wouldn't leave him alone, she decided, and put the kettle on, then turned her attention to her book.

She'd hardly found her place before the doorbell rang. Looking up, she saw Josh's mother outside by the front door, a bunch of flowers in her hand.

Great. Just what she needed, his mother to deal with!

She unfolded her legs and hobbled to the door, wincing as the circulation returned to her feet. 'Mrs Hardy, come in. I'm afraid Josh is in bed, resting. He's only just gone to sleep, but do come in anyway. Would you like a cup of tea? The kettle's just boiled.'

'Thank you, dear, that would be very nice. Oh, and could you put these in water for me?'

She handed the flowers to Fran, who dumped them unceremoniously in the sink and filled it with water. Why did everybody think nurses did flower-arranging as a hobby?

'I'll leave them there for now but, really, you'd do better to do them yourself,' she said with a smile that didn't really reach her eyes. 'I always make a complete pig's ear of flowers.'

'A lady should always be able to arrange flowers,' Mrs Hardy told her reprovingly, and Fran just smiled wider and mashed the tea bags with venom.

'I don't doubt it, but, then, I never pretended to be a lady. Biscuit?'

'I won't, thank you.'

No. Too many calories. Fran took two from the packet, poured the tea into mugs and handed one to Mrs Hardy, before retreating to the sofa and curling up again in her corner.

'So, how is he?' the man in question's mother asked, settling herself cautiously on the other end of the sofa and eyeing Fran in distaste as she dunked her biscuits.

'Tired. Crabby. Sore. He's overdoing it.'

Foolish mistake. Mrs Hardy latched onto it like a terrier with a rat.

'Overdoing it? I thought that's what you were supposed to be here for, to stop him?'

'What am I supposed to do, wrestle him to the ground? He won't stop, and every time my back's turned, he's doing something else. I've told him not to stand on it, but he won't listen. Short of handcuffing him to the bed, I don't see what more I can do.'

Mrs Hardy sighed. 'He's just like his father, never knows when to stop. I'll wait until he wakes, I think, give him a piece of my mind.'

'It could be hours,' Fran warned her, hoping she'd change her mind, but she was adamant.

'No, I've struggled with that dreadful track now. I'll wait until he wakes.'

'In which case,' Fran said, standing up and smiling at her, 'I'll leave him in your capable hands and go shopping.'

'Shopping?'

What imp of mischief had made her do it? 'Yes,' she said blithely, 'Josh has given me his card, and there are some rather nice shops in Woodbridge. I might have a bit of fun. I haven't had any retail therapy for ages.'

Mrs Hardy's eyes narrowed suspiciously, but Fran didn't give her time to speak. Instead, she scooped up her bag and the car keys, thought about struggling with the remote to open the garage door and instead let herself out of the front door.

She'd take the Range Rover, and let Mrs Hardy make of that what she liked.

In fact, she realised when she got down there, she couldn't have got her car out because Isabel, his mother, had parked right in front of the garage door, and if she'd opened it from inside, she would have damaged at least the door and most probably the car as well.

Just as well she hadn't bothered, she thought. Climbing up behind the wheel of the big off-roader, she started the engine, reversed carefully out of the drive and headed for town.

First stop the surgery, she thought, and rummaged in her bag for the letter. She pulled it out and glanced down at it, then braked the car and came to a halt, staring at the name thoughfully.

'Dr Xavier Giraud. Heavens. What a coincidence.'

She'd been meaning to ring him, but she hadn't done so. Would Jackie have done it? She hoped so but, just to be on the safe side, she'd leave him a note at the surgery. Oh, dear. She felt bad about him, but she was too drained, too wrung out to be of any real use to him.

Still, she felt guilty, even though she knew Josh needed her, too, and she couldn't be in two places at once.

She drove into the surgery car park and went inside, to be greeted by the smiling receptionist.

'I've got a letter for Dr Giraud about Joshua

Nicholson. He's had a car accident, and he's a patient of Dr Giraud's.'

'Oh, yes, we heard about it. How is he?'

'Tired. He's come home from hospital too soon, really, ostensibly to rest, but you know what men are like.'

'What are men like?'

The accent, slight though it was, was unmistakable, and she turned, her heart suddenly beating harder, and looked up into a pair of smoke-grey eyes. She held out her hand.

'Dr Giraud, I'm so sorry about yesterday—did Jackie phone you?'

'She did. I believe the lure of young Josh Nicholson was too great.'

Fran smiled ruefully. 'He came in, and he was about to keel over. I figured he was more urgent. I'm so sorry I let you down, though.'

'That's all right, I quite understand. Our loss, his gain. Never mind, Jackie found me someone else, and we'll see how it works out. If not, then maybe when your contract with Mr Nicholson is up you might reconsider us?'

It was a tempting idea, and she gave him a grateful smile. 'Thank you, I'll certainly bear it in mind. And good luck,' she added, for no particular reason.

His eyes locked with hers, a strange expression in them, something tender and approachable that made her almost want to change her mind, but then it was gone and he stepped back with a courteous smile.

'Give Mr Nicholson my regards, and wish him well. If there's any back-up you need from the surgery, or the community nurse to help with anything, don't hesitate to ask.'

'Thank you.'

He nodded, then strode through a door and disappeared, leaving her looking after him thoughtfully.

Had she made a mistake? She didn't know. All she knew was that Josh's mother was getting up a head of steam about her being out with his cashpoint card, and she was going to have deal with it when she got home.

Home? How curious. Just a figure of speech, she told herself briskly. Turning on her heel, she went back out into the car park just in time to see someone reverse into the Range Rover and drive off.

'Oh, damn!' she said, almost stamping her foot, but she managed to get the number, or at least most of it. She inspected the damage with a sinking feeling, and realised it could have been worse, but it was bad enough. Still, at least it was on the same side as the scratches she'd put there, diving into the hedge when that lorry had nearly run her off the road earlier. It could all be fixed at the same time, and then Josh wouldn't be able to complain.

She went to the supermarket, bought most of the things on her list of essentials and went back, to find Josh sitting up in his bedroom with his mother perched on the bed, her weight pulling the quilt so it put pressure on his foot.

As she walked in they stopped talking and turned to look at her, his mother still indignant, Josh curious.

'Bought out Woodbridge?' he asked mildly.

'Absolutely. There was a fabulous suit, but the card wouldn't give me enough. I'll have to take the rest out tomorrow.'

His mouth twitched, but his mother turned to him, enraged. 'Josh! You can't let her get away with it—'

'Mother, she's joking,' he said firmly. 'Look at her. Does she look like a shopaholic?'

Mrs Hardy subsided in some confusion, and Fran tried not to laugh. There wasn't much to laugh about, in fact, so she changed the subject to get the nasty bits over with quickly.

'I took your letter to the surgery, and saw Dr Giraud. He said to give you his regards and if there's anything you need, just shout.' Fran paused. 'And then somebody reversed into your car.'

That wiped the smile off his face, as she'd known it would. 'What?'

'A car in the surgery car park. It just reversed into it, and then drove off. He must have realised, but he didn't stop.'

'Did you get his number?'

'Yes—well, most of it.'

'And make and model, and colour?'

She looked blankly at him. 'It was red.'

'Red. A red what?'

She shrugged. 'I don't know. I don't do cars. A Ford? A Vauxhall? A Renault?'

'Anything, really. Give me the number.'

She pulled the scrap of paper out of her bag and handed it to Josh, and he picked up the phone by the bed and punched in a number. Within seconds he'd been connected to the person in charge, and he gave them all the information she'd been able to come up with.

After a few minutes of one-sided conversation that didn't give Fran much clue as to what was going on, he cradled the phone and looked up at her.

'That's not enough, they don't think. Without more information, it's not possible to pursue it. It's cheaper for them just to pay up—and convenient for you, too.'

'What do you mean?'

'Just that I wonder if it was an accident or if it was one of your errors of judgement that you seemed so confident you'd make when we were at the Jaguar showroom—ricocheting off things, I believe you called it.'

His words hung in the air like frost, stinging her with their slightly mocking insinuation.

'You really think I'd do that—invent a number and a fictitious car, rather than tell you the truth?' She spun on her heel and headed for the door, then paused in the doorway.

'I'm going. You can get your precious mother to look after you—she seems more than happy to do it, and I'm sure she'll do a better job than me!'

She threw her things into her case, dragged them down the stairs from the kitchen and along the corridor to the garage and threw them into her car, then ran back upstairs for the remote control and went back down, pressing the green button to open the garage door.

It started to lift, then there was a thump and a scraping noise, and it ground to a halt.

Mrs Hardy's car. Oh, *hell*!

It was all too much. Hurling the remote across the garage, she sat down on the bonnet of her car, buried her face in her hands and howled.

CHAPTER FIVE

'FRAN?'

She sniffed and scrubbed her cheeks, then lifted her head and glared at Josh.

'What the hell are you doing down here?' she gulped.

'Trying to stop you trashing any more cars?' he said in a mild voice that made her even angrier.

'I didn't trash your car!'

'I know, I know,' he soothed. 'I'm sorry, I was just cross. I'd had my mother sitting in there for half an hour, squashing my foot and telling me how you were running riot in Woodbridge with my credit card. I told her you only had the cashpoint card, but she was insistent that you'd said credit card, and then you came in and told me the car had been hit and I just lost it. I'd spent half the day expecting it to happen, so in a way it wasn't a surprise—'

'Oh, thanks a bunch for the vote of confidence,' she said bitterly. 'Are now you've come down those stairs and walked on your damn leg again, and I think you're doing it just to spite me!'

He laughed softly under his breath then, limping forwards, he reached out and put his arms round her shoulders and drew her against his chest. 'Silly girl.

I'm sorry. Come back inside and calm down. My mother's just going.'

'No doubt with a big hole in the front of her bonnet,' she mumbled into his shirt front.

Josh's chuckle rumbled comfortingly under her ear, and he patted her awkwardly with his plastered hand and stepped back.

'It'll be fine. It's happened before loads of times. It never does very much harm—there's a sensor on the motor. There might be a tiny scratch on the bumper, that's all.'

'She already hates me,' Fran said miserably. 'I don't know what got into me, to tease her about the cashpoint card.'

Josh grinned. 'I don't know, but I thought it was funny. She needs to learn to mind her own business. Come on, let's go back upstairs before I fall over and do something stupid. You can get your bags in a minute. You're not going anywhere.'

'You still want me to stay?'

He looked at Fran in astonishment. 'Of course I do. Who else—my mother? I don't think so.'

She tucked herself under his arm to support him, and together they made their way back along the corridor to the bottom of the stairs.

'You go first,' she told him.

'What, so I land on you and kill you on the way past?'

'So I can shove you up. In fact, why don't you turn

round and sit on your bottom and go up one step at
a time?'

'With one arm? It sounds like hard work.'

'It's better than standing on one leg, and you're
less likely to topple over.'

He grunted, turned and sat down, and then looked
up at her with a grin. 'I hope the camera's not running,' he said, and she glanced up and saw a security
camera pointing towards them. Heavens, the place
was like Fort Knox!

'It'll serve you right. Something to show the grandchildren.'

His face changed, a coldness creeping over it.

'There won't be any grandchildren,' he said crisply,
and hoisted himself up the first step.

Well, now what have I said? she thought to herself.
I'm going to get my jaw wired so I can't talk.
Everything I say seems to be wrong.

She followed him slowly up the stairs, and as they
reached the top she looked over Josh's head and saw
his mother standing there, a disapproving look on her
face.

'I'm sorry about your car,' Fran said quietly. 'I'll
pay for the repairs.'

'With money from my son's account, no doubt.'

'Mother, shut up and go home,' Josh said tiredly.
'We've all had enough for one day and, anyway, it
was your fault. You know you shouldn't park that
close to the garage—it's not the first time it's happened.'

Isabel sniffed and stalked off in a huff, and Josh shook his head and carried on up the last two stairs to the top.

'I'll get your chair,' Fran told him, and squeezed past him, horribly conscious of her tear-stained face and Isabel's disapproval, but there was no sign of her. Maybe she'd let herself out, Fran thought hopefully, but no such luck.

Just as Fran pushed the wheelchair to the top of the stairs, Mrs Hardy appeared behind her, bag in hand.

'I'm going,' she said crisply. 'You'll hear from me about the car. Leave a forwarding address with Joshua.'

'I'll be here,' she said firmly, hoping it was still true.

'Joshua?'

'Goodbye, Mother. I'll ring you.'

'You do that. Oh, and I arranged your flowers. Frances said she couldn't do it.'

'Francesca,' Fran said under her breath, and Josh laughed soundlessly as his mother stalked out.

He pulled himself to his feet and stood swaying slightly in front of Fran. She grabbed his shoulders and steadied him.

'Sit down, for goodness' sake, before you fall,' she chided, and he sat, but not before he'd bent forwards and dropped a brief and totally platonic kiss on her lips.

'Thank you,' he said.

'For what?' she said, her heart jumping about behind her ribs. 'Causing a fight between you and your mother?'

'No. Just being you. Just being here, putting up with me. I'm like a bear with a sore head at the moment. Right now this accident is the last thing I need, and I've got so much I should be doing and it's getting to me. I don't need you to help me fight with my mother, we can manage that all on our own.'

'What sort of things?' Fran asked, concentrating on his worries rather than on the woman who was fast becoming the bane of her life.

'Oh, phone calls to make, paperwork to catch up on—I could do a lot of it lying on the bed or the sofa, but I need the stuff out of my study before I can do it.'

'So ask me, and I can bring it to you. You just need to keep your body still. Your mind can do what it likes, so long as you don't get too stressed—and judging by the sound of it, not being able to do things is more stressful than doing them. So, tell me what you want and where you want it, and I'll bring it to you, but you're going to lie and rest if I have to pin you down.'

Josh smiled, that slow, lazy, sexy smile that he did so well. 'You could always handcuff me to the bed,' he said a little huskily, and she had a sudden and shockingly vivid image of him spreadeagled on the mattress, totally at her mercy.

'In your dreams, sunbeam,' she retorted.

'Oh, yes. Absolutely.'

Hot colour scorched her cheeks, and he laughed softly.

'You're so easy to tease,' he murmured. 'I'm sorry. I should remember my place and not make innuendo. Is that singular or plural, by the way?'

'Heaven knows. Come on, let's get this study sorted out.'

'Before we do that, would you like to go down and shut the garage door?'

Fran's cheeks, just in the process of cooling, heated again. 'I don't know if I can. I threw the remote across the floor,' she confessed unhappily.

'Ah.' One very eloquent brow arched just a tiny bit. 'In that case, perhaps you'd better check it out and I'll get someone here in the morning to deal with it if necessary. There's a keypad on the wall between the doors, by the way, if it is broken, so you can still shut it. Just make sure the remote control isn't in the garden, or someone might be able to open it—oh, and could you put the Range Rover away?'

'You trust me?' she said with only a trace of sarcasm.

Josh sighed and went to ram his right hand through his now almost non-existent hair, and clunked the cast against his head. 'Oh, hell. Yes, you difficult, prickly woman, I trust you. Just go and sort it out for the night, and we'll do a little damage assessment in the morning.'

Fran could hardly wait.

*   *   *

The remote control was fine, to Josh's relief, and so was the garage door. The Range Rover was only slightly scraped, and in amongst the network of scars from her expeditions into the hedgerows yesterday it hardly showed.

With a shrug, he resigned himself to having the whole side resprayed, and decided he'd wait until Fran left. No point in asking for trouble.

'OK, let's go,' he said. Hoisting himself out of the wheelchair, he hitched himself up into the passenger seat, wincing as his pelvis gave him a running commentary on the subtle twisting movement he put it through.

Fran must have seen his face, because she frowned at him. 'Are you all right?'

'Just tweaked something. I'm fine—and don't start the doing-too-much lecture again,' he sighed tiredly.

'I wouldn't dare. It's more than my job's worth,' she muttered, and, stepping back, slammed his door shut.

He winced again and suppressed a smile. Hot-tempered little vixen. She was worse than him when it came to having a short fuse!

She got in beside him, started the car and reversed very carefully and deliberately out of the drive, then crept along the track at about five miles an hour.

'Are you doing that just to be annoying?' he asked, and she shot him a surprised look.

'Doing what? Going slowly so I don't jostle your fractures? I'll go fast if you like.'

Sarky little madam. 'This is fine,' he retorted. So he'd misread her again, and yet again she'd snapped his head off. Oh, well, it was better than her being subservient.

Maybe.

She took him to the gallery, and he slid carefully off the car seat and down to the ground, taking care not to twist this time, and then she pushed him up the makeshift ramp in the doorway and into the building.

'Josh! Good to see you.'

He looked round and caught sight of Angus, the site foreman, coming towards him. 'Angus. How's it going?'

'Good. We had a bit of a hold-up yesterday, waiting for the building inspector, but we've had the go-ahead now on the footings for the dividing wall and the concrete's poured and the wall will be going up tomorrow. We've got some old studwork to make the frame, a bit of oak from a barn that fell down, and I think it'll be very impressive.'

Josh nodded, relieved that things were going well. 'Are we on target for Christmas?' he asked, and Angus grinned.

'Oh, yes. Easy.'

He snorted. 'Not you going out, the public coming in,' he reminded him, and again Angus grinned.

'I know that. It'll be fine. You worry too much.'

He did, but only because he got the distinct feeling

that nobody else ever worried enough. Still, as long as Angus felt that Josh still had his finger on the pulse, he supposed they had more chance of it being completed on schedule.

They checked a few more details, then Josh turned to Fran standing patiently behind him.

'OK, let's roll,' he said. 'I'll see you, Angus. Keep in touch.'

'Will do, boss.'

'So, where to now?' Fran asked, pushing him towards the door.

'Lunch?' he suggested.

'In town, or back home?'

'Home, I think. Time to sort my study out a bit and rig me up a mini-office in the kitchen. I know I made a few phone calls yesterday, but nothing like enough. I've got loads of paperwork to catch up on.'

'Just so long as you don't expect me to type anything,' she warned, but Josh just laughed.

'I talk into the computer—it's clever. I can do it totally hands-free, and it saves all that messing about with one finger.'

So they went back and had lunch, and afterwards Fran wheeled him into the study, helped him find the most important things to start off with and then wheeled him back to the kitchen and settled him on the sofa in a sea of paperwork and electronics.

While he worked she pottered in the kitchen, humming softly to herself, and there was something so cosy and domestic about it that it gave him the shivers.

Hell, he was almost happy about it, that was the most worrying thing!

With a growl of frustration he forced himself to concentrate and not listen to her, but it was hopeless. He couldn't take it any more.

'Do you think you could stop singing?' he said abruptly, and she froze in her tracks and coloured slightly.

'Oh—I'm sorry, I didn't realise I was. Was I distracting you?'

'What do you think?' he growled, and she clamped her lips together on the retort she'd been about to make and said nothing.

Her silence, as they say, spoke volumes.

She banged the chopping board down on the worktop, and chopped and sliced and scraped with terrifying concentration.

'Eye of toad and leg of newt,' he muttered under his breath, and her head snapped round and she glared at him.

'I beg your pardon?'

'Just wondered what you were putting in the cauldron,' he said mildly.

'You, shortly,' she said without missing a beat. 'I'm just making the stock.'

He pressed his lips together to stop the smile, but it escaped anyway, and that, of course, was the wrong thing to do.

'Are you laughing at me?' she demanded, hands on hips.

Lord, she was gorgeous when she was angry. 'Not in the least,' he soothed. 'You just cheered me up, that's all.'

'Well, I'm glad I make you feel better,' she snapped, and attacked a carrot.

He hung onto the smile a bit better this time, and went back to work, ignoring her.

It was still disturbing, though, how even her silence was companionable...

How *dare* he sit there and laugh at her? Ignorant pig. It was a great shame she didn't know any spells. She'd put one hell of a hex on him if she did!

Her anger carried through most of the preparation of the casserole, but by the time she'd finished it she'd calmed down and told herself she was overreacting.

'Right, I'm going outside for a bit of air,' she announced, and looked up, to find that he'd quietly dozed off while she'd been working. Her heart softened and, walking softly up to him, she took the hand-held recorder from him, removed the paperwork from his chest and covered him lightly with a throw that was folded over the end of the sofa.

He looked exhausted, and she wondered how much he was sleeping at night. Less than her, that was certain, because she hadn't heard a sound from him in the past two nights because she'd been out for the count.

She hadn't even had the dream, to her surprise, but she knew it wouldn't be long. Tonight, maybe? Tomorrow? She hoped she wouldn't wake him, but she'd woken her flatmate in the past, so it was quite likely.

Well, she'd cross that bridge when she got to it.

It was three more nights before Fran had the dream, by which time they'd visited the fracture clinic and Josh had been given a crutch to help him move short distances without the wheelchair. The consultant hadn't approved, but it was better than Josh doing it without the support, which was the alternative.

On the way out they'd been narrowly missed by an ambulance coming in with everything blazing, and Fran had felt her heart start to pump and her breathing accelerate.

No, she thought, it's over. I don't have to go through this any more.

But she did, at least in her sleep, and that night she woke screaming and sobbing, scrubbing her arms against the bedclothes to rub off the blood, her heart thundering, tears pouring down her face.

'Fran? Fran, for God's sake, what's wrong?'

The light came on, shockingly bright, and she found she was sitting bolt upright in bed, scrubbing at her arms.

She stopped dead and looked at them, then up at Josh, and then she dropped her face into her hands and sobbed her heart out.

'Oh, Fran, what is it?'

'Just a dream,' she gulped. 'It's nothing. Go back to bed.'

'No. Not while you're like this. Shove up.'

And he peeled back the quilt and climbed in beside her, drew her down into his arms and held her as another wave of weeping swept over her.

'I feel such an idiot,' she mumbled after a while, but he just patted her awkwardly with his good hand and made soothing noises.

'Tell me about it if you like—if it helps. Sometimes it does.'

She didn't think it would, but the images were so clear they weren't going to go away, and perhaps he was right—talking about it might help.

'It's the blood,' she said unsteadily. 'It just gets everywhere, and I can't get rid of it. Everybody's bleeding, and I can't stop them, not all of them, and everywhere I look, there's another body, or another relative screaming and telling me to do something...'

'Is this just the dream, or is this what happened?' he asked her, but she couldn't tell him.

'I don't know. Both. They blur into each other so I can't remember any more what's real and what isn't. It's all the same, though, in the end. I'm helpless, and everybody dies. It's awful.'

'Is that why you gave up your job in A and E? The dreams?'

She shook her head. 'No, the reality. The dreams are just a byproduct, a pale imitation. The real thing

Get FREE BOOKS and a FREE GIFT when you play the...

LAS VEGAS GAME

Just scratch off the gold box with a coin. Then check below to see the gifts you get!

YES!
I have scratched off the gold Box. Please send me my **2 FREE BOOKS** and **gift for which I qualify**. I understand that I am under no obligation to purchase any books as explained on the back of this card.

386 HDL DRQJ   186 HDL DRQY

FIRST NAME	LAST NAME

ADDRESS

APT.#	CITY

STATE/PROV.	ZIP/POSTAL CODE

(H-R-12/02)

7	7	7	Worth TWO FREE BOOKS plus a BONUS Mystery Gift!
🍒	🍒	🍒	Worth TWO FREE BOOKS!
🔔	🔔	♣	TRY AGAIN!

Visit us online at
www.eHarlequin.com

Offer limited to one per household and not valid to current Harlequin Romance® subscribers. All orders subject to approval.

was much, much worse. I used to wait to wake up sometimes but, of course, it didn't happen. So, there. That's what it's like. Every night.'

He reached out and turned off the overhead light, leaving just the dim light from the hallway.

'That must be hell. No wonder you gave up.'

'It was the relatives—the awfulness of having to tell people that there was nothing you could do, and you would be wondering if you still had their son's blood streaked all over your face or if you had washed it off, as you'd intended to. After a time you get hard, or you try, and you make awful jokes, but even so it gets to you in the end.'

'I'm sorry.'

Josh's left hand was moving rhythmically against her shoulder, his right hand resting on her arm as it draped over his chest. It slowly dawned on her that they were in bed together, and that it felt really good—safe. Secure.

Fran swallowed hard. She wanted to feel secure, but she didn't, not at the moment. Too much was in a state of flux in her life, having left the job and the flat, and she felt terribly insecure.

And now suddenly Josh was here, his arms round her, and she could feel the tension draining out of her body, leaving her limp in his arms.

Within minutes, she was asleep.

Josh lay there for ages, listening to the even rhythm of Fran's breathing and soaking up her warmth. It felt so good to lie next to her, but he couldn't stay there, not for the rest of the night—not and retain his sanity.

Once he was sure she was totally out of it, he eased his arm carefully out from under her neck and tucked the pillow there instead, then lifted her arm off his chest and shifted away.

She made a soft, sleepy noise and curled into the warmth where his body had been, and with a sigh of regret he swung his legs over the edge of the bed and stood up, wincing as he did so.

His thigh was throbbing, his pelvis ached and his lower leg was as heavy as lead. There was no way he was going to get back to sleep, he realised, so he went into the kitchen, got a glass of water and shuffled over to the sofa. He'd lie there and do some work, and if he dozed off, so much the better.

He pulled the throw over his legs, picked up the last stack of papers he'd been working on and settled down to go through them, but all he could think about was how she'd felt snuggled up against his side, and how soft and warm her body had been, and how he wanted to protect her.

That scared the spit out of him. He didn't do the whole protective male thing. He didn't believe in it. Women were like his mother—capable and independent—and most of them were hard as nails and not in the least in need of being looked after.

Fran was no exception. She'd just had a rough time. She'd get over it, and if she didn't, perhaps she needed the help of a therapist. She certainly didn't need him protecting her!

CHAPTER SIX

FRAN woke late, feeling refreshed and gloriously rested. She rolled over and opened her eyes, and was stunned by the amount of light streaming in round the curtains. She stared at her watch in horror, and almost catapulted out of bed.

It was half past eight! Josh, she thought, and without stopping to grab her dressing-gown, she ran out of her room and into his bedroom. He wasn't there, his bed was rumpled and empty, and she panicked.

'Josh?'

She ran into his bathroom, dreading what she might find, but it, too, was empty, and so she ran back towards the kitchen, her heart in her mouth.

'Morning.'

She stopped in her tracks and stared at him in astonishment. He was lying on the sofa, the throw over his legs and a pile of paperwork scattered all round him. She put her hands on her hips and glared at him.

'Why aren't you in bed? You gave me the fright of my life. I thought something dreadful had happened to you!'

'I couldn't sleep. I thought I may as well get on with my work.'

'You should have woken me!' she ranted, her heart still banging against her ribs. 'I thought you'd fallen down and broken something!'

'You'd only just gone back to sleep,' he pointed out. 'I don't think you would have thanked me if I'd woken you up to tell you that I couldn't sleep.'

She opened her mouth to speak, but then shut it again. 'You've been here all that time? Since when? I've no idea what time it was.'

He shrugged. 'I don't know—half past two, quarter to three?'

And all that time he'd been working here while she'd been fast asleep. She dragged her hair back off her face, her fingers tangling in it, and hugged her arms round her waist, suddenly conscious of the little nightshirt and just how naked she was underneath it.

'Um, I'll be back in a minute,' she said, and fled back to her bedroom. Grabbing her clean clothes, she ran into the shower-room, washed rapidly and dressed, then ran back to the kitchen.

Josh was smiling slightly mockingly, and she scraped her damp hair back from her face and glowered at him.

'Have you had breakfast?'

'Of course not. How was I supposed to make it? Anyway, I know if I stand up you'll yell at me.'

How did he manage to sound so innocent? He didn't have a problem standing up when it suited him, she thought, and then noticed that the coffee-maker had been on and there was about an inch of thick, black brew in the bottom of the filter jug.

'More coffee?' she asked him with just the same innocence, but he refused to rise.

'No, thanks, I've had plenty.'

'I don't doubt it,' she muttered under her breath, and stomped over to the toaster. 'Toast?'

'Do nicely, thanks. Butter and marmalade.'

'Any time. My pleasure.'

'Please,' he said with only a thread of sarcasm. He put down his hand-held recorder, shuffled his papers together and propped himself up a little in the corner of the sofa, his arms spread out along the back and side. 'So, I take it from your rather tardy appearance this morning that you slept well in the end?'

She turned to look at him, but there was no sarcasm in his voice now, just a genuine, friendly enquiry. Maybe he really did care, she thought. She remembered the feel of him against her, his arms around her, his heart beating steadily under her ear, and her cheeks warmed. 'Yes, thanks. Much better. I'm sorry I disturbed you.'

'I was awake anyway,' he told her. 'My leg was playing me up.'

Her hand flew to her mouth. Painkillers! 'I need to give you a pill—'

'Don't worry, I had one in the night. That's why I made the coffee—you said caffeine enhances the action, and I thought that sounded like a fine idea.'

'You should have woken me,' she repeated, annoyed with him for struggling alone and making her feel guilty. Heaven knows, there was little enough she could do for him in the way of nursing care, and if he was going to insist on taking that over as well, there really was no point at all in her being here.

His toast popped up, and she buttered it, slapped on a good layer of marmalade and cut it into neat little triangles. She handed it to him, and perched on the end of the sofa, watching him.

'I mean it,' she said, cross with him for ignoring her. 'There's no point in me being here if you aren't going to make use of my services.'

Josh choked on the toast, coughing and spluttering and finally coming up for air, his eyes streaming. He waved a hand frantically at her, and she passed him the last inch of cold coffee in his mug. He swallowed it, coughed again and then settled back against the sofa with a wheezy sigh.

'Exactly what services are we talking about?' he said, gasping and chuckling, and she suddenly realised what she'd said that had caused him to choke.

With a growl of frustration, Fran stood up and stalked back to the kitchen. 'Men!' she muttered under her breath. 'Always have to take everything the wrong way.'

She threw two pieces of bread into the toaster and jabbed the lever down, then stood watching it and tapping her foot until it was done. Behind her, she could hear the occasional chuckle. Damn his evil hide, he was enjoying this far too much!

The trouble was, of course, all that proximity last night had totally trashed their professional and distant relationship. Not that it had ever been very professional, she admitted to herself, with all the disagreements that they'd had along the way. Oh, rats. What was the matter with her? She'd always managed to be professional in the past. What was it about this particular man that got so thoroughly under her skin?

Apart from the fact that he was gorgeous, and he had that incredibly sexy smile, and those wicked eyes, and a body to die for, not to mention an outrageous sense of humour and a tremendous sense of fun. On top of that, of course, he was very generous. Witness his sponsorship of Annie, the struggling sculptor.

So, no reason at all really why he should get under her skin. A very boring and ordinary man, what with one thing and another!

She suppressed a little wail of frustration and scraped a streak of butter on her toast, then thought better of it and put more on, then smeared a huge dollop of marmalade over the top.

'So are you making more coffee?' he asked hopefully, and she shot him a baleful look.

'You said no.'

'That was before you tried to choke me.'

'*I* tried to choke you? I like that! *You* were the one who choked, it was nothing to do with me. It's your perverted mind.'

'My mind isn't in the least bit perverted,' he corrected mildly, 'and, anyway, it's hardly my fault if I had to spend an hour pressed up against your un-questionable charms.'

'Don't force yourself,' she retorted. 'I never asked you to get into bed with me!'

'No, you just howled your eyes out and looked dev-astated,' he said quietly. 'What the hell was I sup-posed to do, leave you to it? You looked awful.'

Fran turned away, unable to meet his eyes any longer. 'I know. I'm sure I looked a real fright. Thanks for being there for me.'

'You're welcome. I could say it was my pleasure, but you'd no doubt misinterpret it.'

She gave him a rueful smile. 'I'm sorry, I'm doing it again, aren't I? Jumping down your throat for every little thing.'

'Forget it. Can we start again? Good morning.'

Her smile softened. 'Good morning,' she echoed. 'Would you like some coffee?'

'That would be lovely, thank you,' he murmured, his eyes shimmering with laughter. 'And then I've got a suggestion to make.'

'Oh?' She poured the coffee and took it over to him, perching by his feet and watching him curiously. 'What's that?'

'I could do with going to London. I know you've just got away from there, but I could do with dropping in to see my accountant and having a look in a couple of galleries for ideas, and then I thought maybe we could go to a show.'

'That's an awful lot for one day!' she said, horrified, but Josh just chuckled.

'Not in one day, Fran. I've got a flat down there. We could stay there and do a couple of things a day—take a week, if necessary. What do you say?'

She stared thoughtfully at him. 'Where's the flat?'

'Just off Tavistock Square,' he told her. 'Right near Oxford Street. You could go shopping.'

Fran gave a wry snort of laughter. 'I lived in London for years. I could shop any time I wanted to—but I wouldn't mind going round some galleries with you, and the show sounds fun.'

He grinned, and her heart hiccuped against her ribs, but she told herself not to be so ridiculous. Josh was her patient, and she'd already just given herself a severe talking-to about professionalism after allowing him to spend part of the night with her.

And look how you felt! her alter ego reminded her with ruthless efficiency.

That was different, though, she argued back. I'd had a nightmare. He was comforting me.

And you loved every second of it. So much for being professional.

'You don't think I'll overdo it?'

She smiled. 'Not if I have anything to say about it. I'm sure you'll be fine. You could do with a bit of light relief, I think, and I know I certainly could. So—let's do it!'

It was strange, Fran thought, that she'd lived in London for years and had never really enjoyed herself

before. Josh took her to places she'd never even
known existed—tiny little galleries tucked away off
New Bond Street, and intimate little restaurants where
they all seemed to know him. They didn't go to a
show, because by the evenings he seemed to flag, but
she didn't mind at all. Instead, they would sit in his
flat with a glass or two of wine, and either watch
something on television or listen to music.

There was something cosily romantic about it,
something strangely intimate. They'd talk about what
they'd seen and the galleries they'd been to, and
which exhibitions had worked and why. Then she'd
help him into bed and arrange a pillow by his leg to
keep the weight off it, and he'd thank her, and something would hang in the air between them, some
strange electric charge that seemed to crackle through
the air and steal her breath away.

And then he'd say goodnight, in that soft, gruff
voice, and she'd go into her room and lie there with
her heart pounding and wonder why she'd chosen to
fall in love with a man so far out of her reach.

Still, there was one good thing about it. She was
so busy thinking about Josh that she didn't have a
nightmare again, not in the three nights they were
there, but then when they were driving home on the
Friday they passed the spot where Josh had had his
accident, and he told Fran a little more about how it
had happened.

'All I can remember is that it was a really dark

night, and suddenly I saw this shape looming up in front of me, coming right at me, and at the last moment I realised it was a horse. I suppose I swerved to avoid it, but I didn't really know any more about it until they were trying to cut me out of the car. I remember that. I can remember the pain, and everybody being very calm and reasonable, but I didn't feel very calm and reasonable, I just wanted to get out.'

'Were you trapped long?' she asked, only too able to picture the scene.

Josh shrugged. 'I don't remember, they said about three quarters of an hour. I know they didn't want it to be too long—something to do with crush injuries.'

'Crush syndrome,' she told him. 'Protein in the blood. It messes up the kidneys.'

'Whatever. They got me out, and after that it's all a bit patchy for a few days. I guess I was drugged up to the eyeballs.'

'Very likely. Still, you're doing well now.'

He rolled his eyes. 'If you say so,' he said with a sigh. 'Progress feels frustratingly slow sometimes.'

'You just expect too much of yourself. It's only three weeks. You ought to try some relaxation.'

Predictably, he didn't think much of that. 'You'll have me chanting mantras next,' he said disgustedly.

Fran laughed. 'Patience isn't really your strong suit, is it?'

She didn't need to look at him, she could feel the scorching sarcasm of that cobalt blue gaze. Her lips twitched, and she pressed them together to stop herself from laughing.

After a moment, she heard him chuckle. 'How the hell do you do it? You push my buttons every single time.'

'Years of practice. I have a brother,' she told him with a smile. 'I've been teasing him since before I could speak.'

'Poor bugger,' Josh said with a soft laugh. 'He has my sympathy.'

'I'm sure he doesn't need it—he used to thrash the living daylights out of me.'

His chuckle was infectious, and they ended up laughing together and swapping childhood stories. It was fine until she mentioned his parents. That was when he grew quiet, and she could have kicked herself. Of course, his mother had a different name, so either they were divorced or his father was dead, which she didn't think he was. Mrs Hardy had said something about him being like his father, and it hadn't sounded as if he was in the past tense.

So, divorced, then. Was that anything to do with Josh's odd remark about grandchildren the other day, when he'd withdrawn into himself and gone so cold and distant for a minute? Had his parents put him off marriage? It was something that not even she, with her consummate lack of tact, could ask him. If he wanted her to know, he'd volunteer the information.

He didn't, and indeed he hardly spoke again that day. They got home as the last rays of sun were dying over the River Deben, and after a light supper Josh said he was ready for bed.

'I could do with an early night,' he confessed, and he did look tired. Too much too soon, Fran thought, and wondered if she should have slowed him down in London and made him do less.

How?

Handcuff him to the bed, as he'd suggested?

He was in the bathroom, fortunately, so he didn't see the soft colour flood her cheeks, or see her pick up his pillow and bury her face in it, breathing deeply.

The cleaning team had been in, though, and all she got was a whiff of fabric softener.

'You're an idiot,' she told herself, and put the pillow down hastily, turning back the quilt and tucking the support pillow in at the bottom.

A moment later Josh came out of the bathroom, limping and leaning heavily on the one crutch he was able to use, and she helped him into bed, gave him his pills and made sure his leg was comfortable.

'All right?' she asked softly, and he nodded.

'Yes, I'm fine. Glad to be back home.' He reached out and caught her hand, the edge of the cast feeling rough against her fingers. 'Thanks, Fran. You've been a real star the past few days, driving me round London. It's been fun, hasn't it?'

She swallowed hard. 'Yes—yes, it has. I just hope I haven't let you get overtired.'

He gave a soft huff of laughter. 'I'm a big boy,

Fran. I'm twenty-eight. I can work out for myself when I'm tired.'

'It takes time to get used to it when you've been injured. You expect to be able to do more than you can. I should be helping you adjust to that.'

'And you are. Believe me, you nag me quite enough. Now, go to bed and rest, and I'll see you in the morning. Sleep well.'

He pressed her fingers to his lips, then released her, and she turned off his light and went to bed, her fingers still tingling from his kiss.

She didn't sleep, though, at least not for a while. She thought about his parents, and then the accident, and when she finally drifted off, it was to a tangled dream of chaos and confusion, people crying, a small boy lying there begging for her help. And then suddenly he was Josh, and he was trapped in a car, pleading for her help, but she couldn't help him, and he was going to die—

'Fran? Fran, it's OK. It's a dream. Wake up.'

She dragged in a few gulps of air and opened her eyes, to find Josh sitting on the edge of her bed. She blinked against the light, and he turned it off, watching her in the half-light from the landing.

'OK now?'

She nodded, then shook her head. 'You were dying,' she whispered shakily. 'You were trapped in the car, and I couldn't help you, and you were bleeding to death...'

'Oh, Fran, I'm fine. I'm sorry, I shouldn't have told

you about the accident, that was so stupid. Here, go to sleep. I'll stay with you—move over.'

So she wriggled across the bed, and he slid in beside her, wrapped his good arm around her and rocked her gently against his chest. The last echoes of his cries in her nightmare were still going through her, leaving her trembling and gasping, dry sobs tearing at her throat.

'It was so real,' she whispered.

'I know.'

She tipped her head back, looking up at him in the gloom, and their eyes locked.

'What am I going to do with you?' he murmured.

There was a long, aching silence, and then with an untidy sigh he lowered his mouth to hers. The kiss, as kisses go, was brief, but as he lifted his head and looked down at her, something changed.

'Fran?' he said softly, and then his mouth was on hers again, searching hungrily. He shifted, rolling her onto her back, and his mouth slanted over hers and consumed her.

Nobody, she thought in a daze, nobody had *ever* kissed her like that before, as if they were dying for her. His fingers cupped her jaw, the cast grazing the delicate skin, and his lips traced paths all over her face, sipping, sucking, nibbling the soft skin under her ear, and then with a sigh he found her mouth again and plundered it.

His body was hard against hers, needy and urgent, and she arched against him, wanting more—much,

much more. Then he lifted his head, his breathing ragged, and looked down at her with blazing eyes.

'Fran, if we're going to do anything more about this, you're going to have to help me,' he said raggedly. 'And if we're not, I'd better get the hell out of your bed right now.'

'But—we can't. Your leg…'

'My leg's miles away,' he said.

'Are you sure?'

'Yes, I know exactly where it is,' he assured her, and she laughed, a breathless little sound that broke the tension a fraction.

'There's something else we ought to think about,' she said, worrying.

'In my bedside drawer.'

She slid out of bed and went through to his room, and there in the top drawer was a new packet of condoms. She fingered them thoughtfully. So much for maintaining a professional distance, she thought, but she didn't want to and, anyway, they'd already gone far beyond that.

Picking up the packet, she shut the drawer and went back to him.

'Found them?'

'Yes. Josh, are you sure you're ready for this? I don't want to hurt you.'

He was lying on his back, his left arm flung up above his head, and his slow, lazy smile nearly finished her. 'Oh, I'm ready,' he said huskily. 'I'm so ready I think I'm going to die if you don't get back into this bed right now.'

'I'm so scared I'll hurt you.'

'You won't. It'll be fine. Fran, please, stop worrying and get back into bed before I blow a fuse.'

Her heart thumped against her ribs, and she slid in beside him on his good side, careful not to hurt his leg. 'Josh, kiss me again,' she whispered, suddenly unsure, and he lifted himself up on his elbow and lowered his mouth to hers.

'Oh, I intend to,' he murmured against her lips. 'I fully intend to...'

Whatever fears or doubts she had then disappeared out of the window. His mouth coaxed her, heating her blood, making her heart pound and heat pool in her.

'Josh, please,' she begged, and he rolled to his back.

'I thought you'd never ask,' he rasped, and in the almost dark she could see his eyes glittering with need. 'Just—be careful.'

'I'll be gentle,' she vowed. 'Tell me if I hurt you.'

She moved across him, lowering herself to him with infinite care, and a deep, ragged groan rose from his throat. 'Oh, Fran,' he murmured unsteadily. 'That feels so good...'

She couldn't speak. Emotion was choking her, emotion and sensation and a terrible, raging need that was going to consume her. She moved against him, taking him deeper, and shock waves rippled outwards, burning her up in a wild fire that was going to consume her.

'Josh,' she cried brokenly, and he pulled her down against his chest, holding her close as the storm crashed around them.

And then it was over, the waves of passion receding, and she lay against him, his arms cradling her, and wept.

She wept because she loved him and she knew it would never come to anything, but she knew that she'd touched heaven with him, and nothing in her world would ever be the same again...

'Fran?'

She opened her eyes and found Josh lying there, his face mere inches from hers, his eyes tender.

'Morning,' she said softly, suddenly shy.

'Happy birthday,' he said.

Her heart filled with joy. 'You remembered! I didn't think you would.'

'Of course I remembered. I wouldn't dare forget. You'd accuse me of overdoing it and getting amnesia...'

She punched his shoulder lightly and he laughed and leant forwards and kissed the tip of her nose.

'I could use the bathroom,' he told her. 'My teeth need cleaning, and I could do with a shower. Fancy joining me?'

A slow smile played over her mouth. 'Sounds good. Let me help you into the bathroom, and I'll put the coffee on and heat up the oven for breakfast. I've got some croissants in the freezer—fancy them?'

'Later,' he murmured. 'Shower first.'

'Oh, yes,' she vowed.

She gave him a few minutes of privacy, then tapped on the bathroom door.

'Can I come in?'

'Of course you can come in.'

He was standing at the basin, his face covered in shaving foam, and she went up behind him and slid her arms round him, resting her cheek against the firm, smooth skin of his back. He rinsed his face, blotted it roughly dry and turned to her with a smile.

'Better?'

'I liked the stubble.'

He rolled his eyes. 'There's no pleasing some women,' he teased, and held out his arm. 'Bin bag?'

'All ready.' She put his arm in it, taped it on and helped him across the room to the shower. He was already naked, but she wasn't, and he hadn't seen her before, not in the cold, hard light of day. Suddenly shy, she peeled off her nightshirt and dropped it on the floor, avoiding his eye.

'Let me look at you,' he said gruffly, and she turned towards him, her heart pounding.

He lifted his left hand and slowly, thoughtfully traced a path down her throat, over her breasts and down to her navel.

'You're beautiful,' he said gruffly. 'I thought you would be.'

She shook her head, but he anchored her chin with his fingers and lifted her face up to his. 'Yes, you are,' he told her in a voice that brooked no argument. 'Why can't you take a compliment, Fran? Was it that bastard that slept with your flatmate?'

She shrugged. 'Him and others.'

'Others? What others?'

'Oh, I don't know. Men all tell you what they think you want to hear, to get their way.'

'Women do the same, you know. You need to learn to tell the difference between hollow flattery and genuine admiration—and you are beautiful.'

She met his eyes, and the look in them no way qualified as hollow flattery. She felt warmth spreading through her, and she smiled softly.

'Thank you,' she said quietly. 'That's the nicest thing anybody's ever said to me.'

Josh chuckled. 'That makes a change, for you to think I said something nice.'

'It makes a change for you to do it,' she teased. 'Come on, I'm getting cold. Let's shower.'

It was amazing what he could do from the chair, Josh thought. He'd lathered Fran all over, and then had sat her on his good knee and kissed her. His hand had found her warm, secret places and she'd writhed against him, soft gasps and eager cries coming from her open mouth.

She'd come for him, her body shuddering, and he'd nearly lost it. Then she'd washed him and returned the favour, and now they were in the bedroom and he wanted her again.

'Fran?'

'What do you want to wear?'

'Nothing. Come here.'

She turned towards him and stopped in her tracks. 'Oh,' she said, colouring prettily.

'Come to bed with me,' he said, holding out his hand, and she crossed the room slowly and took his hand.

'Are you sure?'

'Do I look unsure?'

She glanced down and laughed softly. 'Not really.' She went up on tiptoe and kissed him, and then threw back the quilt and eased him down against the cool sheet.

There was no foreplay. They didn't need any. Their eyes locked together, their hands meshed, and their bodies moved in unison, striving for the same urgent goal.

Josh felt the ripples start inside her, felt the first shudder run through her, and then the deep pulse of his release erupted through him and he was lost.

CHAPTER SEVEN

'So, BIRTHDAY girl, what would you like to do to-day?'

Beside him, Fran stretched lazily. She was warm and comfortable, and she felt more thoroughly loved than she'd ever felt in her life. She couldn't imagine anywhere she'd rather be or anything she'd rather do.

'Do we have to do anything?' she asked.

Josh's low chuckle rumbled through her. 'Not really, not if you don't want to. We ought to get up later, though, because I've got a surprise for you.'

Fran sat bolt upright and looked down at him, delighted. 'You have? I love surprises.'

'Now, why doesn't that surprise me?' he said with a slow grin. 'So, are you going to change your mind about getting up?'

'Oh, yes! Where are we going?'

'Not far. About ten miles. I said we'd ring before we left.'

'I'll go and put the croissants in the oven,' she said, almost bouncing out of bed. 'Stay there, I'll be back in a minute.'

She hurried into the kitchen, put the croissants on an oven tray and went back to find him heading for the bathroom, leaning on the crutch. She was glad to see him using it, because he was much too inclined to try and manage without. Still, maybe all the nagging had finally paid off.

'Do you need a hand?'

He shook his head. 'No, thanks, I can manage.'

By the time he came out, she was washed and dressed and back in the kitchen, piling the hot croissants into a basket.

'Smells good,' he said, sniffing appreciatively.

She eyed him up and down. 'I think there's something missing,' she teased.

'I hope not,' he said with a lazy smile. 'But I could do with some clothes on.'

'Formal or informal?' she asked him.

'Oh, informal, definitely,' he said. 'Jeans and that blue cashmere sweater, I think.'

Fran helped him to dress, thinking that her idea of informal and his were wildly different. The cashmere sweater alone probably cost more than her entire wardrobe, or at least a good chunk of it. Ah, well. Just another reason why this whole thing was such a bad idea, but it was her birthday today, and she wasn't going to think about it.

It was nearly noon before they left, and he directed her through the forest at Butley to a tiny terraced house at the edge of the village.

'Is this it?' Fran asked him in puzzlement.

Josh just smiled that enigmatic smile, and opened the car door. 'I think I'll just use the crutch—there isn't enough room inside for the wheelchair.'

She got out of the car and went round to help him out, and before they were halfway up the path, the door flew open and a tiny, tattered sprite daubed with paint and smelling of turps came bouncing down the path and flung her arms round Josh.

He disentangled her gently and held her at arm's length, smiling down at her with open affection. Then they both turned to look at Fran.

'Fran, I'd like you to meet Annie. Annie, this is Fran. I told you about her on the phone.'

Annie held out a grubby but surprisingly strong little hand and shook Fran's hand in a formal greeting that was nevertheless spontaneous. 'Hi, Fran,' she said cheerfully. 'Come on in, I've put the kettle on. Oh, it's so nice to see you again, Josh! You look much better, you looked really awful in hospital.'

'I felt really awful in hospital,' Josh told her dryly. 'Anyway, Fran's been looking after me.'

She led them through the front door, into the surprisingly bright and open interior. The room occupied the entire ground floor of the cottage, with stairs winding up in one corner, and the whole room was a sea of artwork. Pictures hung on every available piece of wall, they were propped around the floor and stacked five deep against the walls, and in the middle were more of her strange, tortured metal figures.

Oh, heavens, Fran thought, I hope he's not going to buy me one of them for my birthday, because goodness knows what I'll do with it.

'Coffee would be really great, Annie,' Josh said to the young woman, and while she was busying herself with the kettle, Josh turned to Fran. 'I know you like her pictures, so I thought you might like to choose one for your birthday. If there's nothing you like, don't, for goodness' sake, just be polite. And I know you don't like her little people.'

The smile was crinkling the corners of his eyes, and she smiled back ruefully. 'I didn't mean to be unkind,' she said very quietly.

'I know. But you do like the paintings. She did the ones in the hall.'

She hadn't known that but, looking around her now, she could see that it was true. And he was going to buy her one for her birthday? How wonderful!

'Here you go, two coffees.' Annie handed them their mugs, and then stood back with a grin. 'Right, where do you want to start?'

Fran shrugged. 'At the beginning?' she said with a smile.

So Annie started at one end of the room, and picture by picture she went through all the piles. Fran shook her head. She wanted them all. How on earth could she choose?

And then she saw it. It was a picture of the river, painted from Josh's house. At least, she assumed it was, because it captured that wonderful, slightly ethereal atmosphere only too well.

'That's it!' she exclaimed. 'That's the one. Oh, I *love* it!'

'Sure?'

She nodded at Josh. 'Oh, yes, definitely—well, if that's all right? It's awfully big.'

'I painted it from his house one day,' Annie told her. 'I'd been there for the night, because my stove was broken and it was freezing here and Josh wouldn't let me stay, and I got up really early and went outside and painted it, because it was just so gorgeous. He got really mad with me because I got so cold but, like I said to him, I'm used to it. I never have any money for wood, even when the stove isn't broken, so it doesn't really matter.'

She lifted the huge picture off the wall and handed it to Fran. 'Here, I want you to have it. And, no, Josh,' she said, turning to him, 'I won't take any money for it. I owe you so much, much more than I can ever tell you, and it's just a picture. Please. Let it be my present. It's just so nice to be appreciated.'

Fran opened her mouth to protest, then shut it, handed the picture to Josh and hugged Annie impulsively. 'Thank you,' she said, choked. 'Thank you so much. I'll treasure it.'

Josh shook his head slowly from side to side, but she could see he was pleased.

So was Annie, she realised, and so was she. What a wonderful birthday present.

'So, now we've got that done, how's the gallery coming on?' Annie asked him, perching on the edge of a lumpy old sofa.

Josh sat, very cautiously. 'Slowly but surely,' he said. 'Angus assures me it will be done in time, and it will, if I have to go in there and finish it myself.'

Fran rolled her eyes and put her hand on his shoulder. 'Listen to the man talk,' she said laughingly.

'I should believe him, if I were you,' Annie said. 'I've never known him let anything beat him yet.'

Josh snorted rudely. 'I shouldn't be too sure. I think I've met my match in Fran. You wouldn't believe how bossy she is.'

But there was an affectionate note in his voice, and his eyes were tender, and Fran just smiled down at him and couldn't believe her luck.

'Right, we need to go. Annie needs to concentrate. And, Annie, thank you. Just do me another big favour, eh? Lots of stuff for the opening exhibition. We'll come up and help you sort it out.'

Annie's eyes went automatically to the big picture propped up against Fran's leg. 'Um…can we include that? I had intended to.'

'Of course,' Fran agreed instantly. 'Just so long as it's marked ''Not For Sale''! I don't intend to part with it, ever.'

Even though I have nowhere to put it yet, she thought with another little flicker of worry. Still, there was no immediate urgency. Josh would still need her for a couple more weeks, at least.

And then? a little voice asked, but she refused to listen to it, not on such a perfect day. It was her birthday, and she refused to spoil it.

What was that saying? Don't borrow trouble, it'll find you soon enough, or something like that.

Josh stood up, wincing a little. 'Annie, we need to go and let you get on. I can see you're busy.'

'Never too busy to see you. If it wasn't for you, I'd have nothing.'

'Nonsense,' Josh murmured, but Fran had a feeling it wasn't. She put her painting in the back of the Range Rover, and then helped Josh into the seat.

'You will come again soon, won't you? We need to sort out the exhibition stuff. I don't know what I've got that's worth exhibiting.'

'All of it,' Josh told her firmly. 'You could easily fill the gallery, but I want to save some for your next exhibition, and I thought I might take some down to a London gallery I saw this week. You wait and see, Annie. It'll come. Just be patient.'

She smiled uncertainly, and he reached out and hugged her with his left arm. 'Thanks for the picture. You didn't need to do that.'

'Yes, I did,' she replied, and hugged him briefly before stepping back and closing the door. She lifted her hand in a little wave and Fran drove off, still smiling.

'She's a sweetie.'

'She's mad. She's too generous for her own good.'

'Mmm. Maybe that's why you get on so well,' Fran suggested, and he laughed.

'Well, I'd like to be generous, but I've been thwarted,' he said wryly. 'I thought I'd got your present sorted out, but now I haven't. What can I give you?'

Fran smiled at him. 'I thought you'd already given me my birthday present,' she said softly, and his eyes darkened.

'I'm not quite sure who did the giving on that one,' he replied, his voice slightly husky. 'I could have sworn I did a hell of a lot of receiving.'

Fran felt herself colour, and looked quickly back to the road. The last thing he needed was another car accident!

'So, where to, boss?' she asked.

'Home?'

Had the word always sounded so wonderful, or was

it just now, because Josh's home was the only one in the world that mattered to her any more?

'Home sounds good,' she said.

'And then we can check out that birthday present thing again, see who's doing all the giving and make sure the balance is right.'

Her breath jammed in her chest, and she laughed softly.

'Home it is.'

The doorbell rang, and Fran stirred against his side.

'Wake up, sleepyhead. You need to answer that.'

'Let them go away,' she mumbled into his shoulder. 'Can't move.'

'Yes, you can. Come on.' He prodded her, and she groaned and crawled out of bed, snagging his dressing-gown from the back of the door in passing.

'It had better not be your mother,' she said warningly, but he just laughed and rolled onto his back and watched her go.

It wasn't his mother. It was a delivery boy, almost totally concealed behind the biggest arrangement of flowers Fran had ever seen in her life except on her grandmother's coffin, and he peered at her round the side.

'Miss Williams?'

She dragged the neck of Josh's dressing-gown closed and nodded. 'Yes?'

'These are for you. Have a nice day.'

She took them, staggering slightly at the weight of them, and carried them through to the kitchen. There was a card inside, addressed to 'The World's Best

Nag', and she opened the envelope with a smile and read the card.

'Fran. Happy Birthday. Hope this redresses the balance. Josh.'

She chuckled. In terms of weight and volume it certainly did, and the flowers were beautiful. The colours all went really well with the kitchen breakfast room, and she set the arrangement down on the coffee-table, totally swamping it, and stood back.

'Oh, they are gorgeous,' she said softly, feeling her eyes fill. It was eleven years since anyone had given her flowers on her birthday, when her father had brought her home roses for her sixteenth. No other man had ever done such a thing, and she felt quite overwhelmed.

With a little hiccuping sob she ran back to Josh and threw herself into his arms.

'Thank you,' she said into the hollow of his neck, and he lifted her up and looked at her, a smile playing round his mouth.

'I take it they've arrived, then,' he said, and she nodded.

'They're in the breakfast room. They practically fill it. Whatever did you order?'

'A truly huge arrangement,' he said with a smile.

'Well, they got it right—and there was nothing wrong with the balance, it was perfect.'

'Oh,' he said, laughter teasing at his eyes. 'Does that mean you owe me?'

Fran snorted. 'In your dreams. Come and have a look,' she ordered, and all but dragged him out of bed.

He limped up the corridor behind her, and then stopped in the doorway and let his breath out on a low whistle.

'Well. They're pretty big,' he said, laughing.

'They're beautiful—and you were quite right to get an arrangement, I'm useless with flowers.'

'Mmm. You've probably been too busy doing more useful things to have time to learn, although my mother probably wouldn't agree. Still, she's never had to earn her living, so she wouldn't, would she? She's never had anything better to do except play bridge and golf and go out to lunch.'

He put his arms round her from behind and hugged her. 'Talking of which, any chance of some lunch?'

'It's nearly four o'clock.'

'Tea? Got any cakes?'

She turned round in his arms. 'No. And I can't make cakes either. Sorry.'

'Useless. What can you do? Oh, yes. Nag—and drive me crazy with that beautiful, amazingly sexy body. Forget the cakes. We can buy cakes. In fact, why don't I take you out for tea, or would you rather have dinner?'

She laughed, happier than she'd ever been in her life. 'Tea would be lovely—but you might need to get dressed. You seem to be naked again.'

He tapped her on the nose. 'That, witch, is because somebody stole my dressing-gown.'

'So they did,' she said cheekily. 'Just imagine that.'

They went to a hotel for tea, and she didn't know what he said to them but they produced a little cake with a candle on it and sang 'Happy Birthday' to her,

and she blushed and laughed and blew out the candle
and wondered if anyone had ever had such a perfect
birthday before.

Josh was tired the next day. He woke Fran, stirring
restlessly in his sleep as the light began to filter round
the curtains, and she thought he was probably in pain.

She slipped quietly out of bed and brought him a
glass of water and a painkiller, and sure enough he
drifted to the surface a moment later and swore softly
under his breath.

'Are you hurt?' she murmured, and he nodded.

'My leg's giving me hell,' he told her drowsily.

'Take this.'

He propped himself up on one elbow and took it
from her, draining the glass of water before flopping
back on the pillows with a grunt of pain. 'Thanks.'

'You go back to sleep now,' she said, and with a
small assenting noise he settled down again beside
her and soon drifted off. She lay beside him for a
while, thinking over the events of the previous day,
and then, unable to sleep again, she slipped out of
bed and left his room, pulling the door to behind her.

She showered quickly, pulled on her clothes and
went into the kitchen. She needed a cup of tea, and
while it brewed she sat curled up on the sofa, staring
at her lovely flowers.

Her picture was propped up on the breakfast table
at the other side of the room, and she admired it as
well and wondered what she'd done to get so lucky
so suddenly.

It wouldn't last, she thought. Every time she'd

thought things were going well, they'd gone wrong. Why should this be any different?

There had been her job—a successful nursing sister in a busy accident and emergency department, a highly skilled member of a well-honed team—until it had all fallen apart. Then there had been her flatmate, fine at first, then gradually doing less and less, becoming dirtier and untidier by the day until it had been impossible to tolerate and Fran had had to clear up after her so she hadn't gone mad.

Then there had been the boyfriend—nothing serious, nothing like this, and yet she'd thought he'd been hers. She'd thought they'd had some commitment, but it seemed yet again she'd been wrong.

Was she wrong, too, about Josh? Was he just playing with her, trifling with her emotions, amusing himself with her company? He was bored, heaven knows, and she was sure he was used to having women fall at his feet.

Was she just another one of those endless women? Would she, one day, get a gift of jewellery to pay her off? That was what rich men did, wasn't it, when they grew bored of their playthings? They bought them jewellery and gave them the golden goodbye.

Even the thought of it sent a shaft of pain through her, and today, in the cold light of dawn, she let herself think about what she would do when it was over.

Work for Dr Giraud?

'Xavier,' she said. It was pronounced Zavi-ay, in the French way. It was an interesting name. Interesting man, she thought, with kind eyes, and he would have presented no kind of a threat to her sanity.

Well, not in the way Josh did, with his brash humour and quick temper and lazy sexuality.

She realised the kettle had boiled long ago, and she
got up and made herself a cup of tea, then settled
back down with it on Josh's sofa, her feet tucked
under her bottom, and stared into her painting.

It was wonderful, and whatever happened it would
always remind her of Josh.

Her eyes filled with tears, and she dashed them
away angrily. Nothing had happened yet. Maybe it
never would. Unlikely, but stranger things had happened, and there would be plenty of time to be miserable then without getting into it now. She may as
well enjoy the present and all it brought, and let the
future take care of itself.

She'd get there all too soon, that much was certain,
and for now she had Josh.

Putting her mug back down on the corner of the
coffee-table, she snuggled down under the throw and
dozed off...

It was a strange house—one of those houses that
changed from one thing to another as you walked
through it. That was the way with dreams, of course,
but they always seemed so plausible at the time.

She went in through a big door in the middle, with
a fanlight over the top, and the floor of the hall was
tiled in black and white, laid in a diagonal check with
a square border round the edges. It was an old house,
Georgian probably, and as she went in a man walked
towards her, his hand held out to her—not as if to

shake it but to give her something, or to take her hand in his and lift it to his lips.

He murmured something, and his voice was strangely musical, slightly foreign. French?

She couldn't see his face, but there was a dignity and quiet reserve about him that touched her heart.

And then she saw his eyes, the eyes of a soul in torment, and she reached out to him...

Fran was woken by the phone, a sudden, harsh sound in the stillness, and for a moment she didn't know where she was. She looked around, puzzled, and then it all fell into place and she reached out for the handset on the table at the end.

'Hello?'

'Ah, you're still there.'

She sighed mentally and curled up at the other end of the sofa, phone in hand. 'Good morning, Mrs Hardy. I'm sorry, Josh is asleep. Can I get him to call you when he wakes?'

'No. Actually, it was you I rang to talk to. I wanted—well, to apologise,' she said stiffly. 'I'm sorry I was so rude the other day.'

Fran stared at the phone in utter amazement. Had Josh threatened his mother?

'Um, well, actually, so am I,' Fran confessed. 'I shouldn't have teased you about the cashpoint card. It was very unkind—and I'm terribly sorry about your car.'

'Oh, the car's fine,' Mrs Hardy said dismissively. 'You can't even see it. Roger's polished the mark out of the bumper and it's completely gone. And anyway, as Josh pointed out, it's not the first time. You'd think I would have learned.'

'Not necessarily,' Fran said with a sigh. 'Sometimes people make the same mistake over and over again.'

'Well, I certainly have with Josh's garage doors. I'll try and steer clear of them in future.' Her voice changed, becoming softer, almost pleading. 'Tell me, Francesca, how is he?'

She thought of him, lying asleep in his bed exhausted from their love-making, and smiled.

'He's doing fine,' she told Isabel. 'Getting better all the time. He's done rather a lot the past few days, though, because we've been to London, but he's resting now and I'm going to make sure he takes it easy for a few days.'

His mother snorted, sounding curiously like him in a more ladylike way. 'Well, I wish you joy. I've never been able to make him slow down, and with the gallery due to open in a few weeks and the exhibitions to prepare for, he'll be like a cat on a hot tin roof. Can I give you a word of advice? Don't try and slow him down, but go with him, make it easier, help him wherever you can, because he'll keep going until all the jobs are done. If you can do some of them for him, he'll be finished sooner.'

It was sound advice and, coming from his mother who probably knew him better than he'd like to admit, no doubt based on a solid foundation of years of experience of her son's foibles.

'I'll bear it in mind,' she promised, filing it all away for future reference. 'I don't know when he'll wake up,' she went on, 'but he's so tired I really want to leave him to wake naturally. Shall I get him to call you when he surfaces?'

'Only if he wants to,' Mrs Hardy said, and suddenly Fran felt quite sorry for her. She obviously adored her son, but it was equally obvious that they rubbed each other up the wrong way the whole time.

Too different? Or too much alike?

She didn't know. A few days ago she would have said different. Now she wasn't so sure. They both had short fuses and jumped to conclusions, and they both had quick and slightly acid tongues.

The only major difference she could see was that Josh had a sense of humour, and so far there was no sign of his mother even cracking a real smile. There was no doubting that she loved him, though, and Fran found herself promising to ring and update her on his progress, because they both knew that he wouldn't, given a choice.

Then she cradled the phone and sat there, the remnants of her dream dissolving around her like the mist over the river in Annie's painting, and she frowned.

She couldn't remember it, just isolated fragments, little bits and pieces that didn't make sense, and yet the dream had all been quite logical.

Shaking her head, she stood up. She'd make a fresh pot of tea, get her book from the bedroom and settle down for a read. If Josh was going to start running round flat out, with her chasing after him trying to slow him down, she may as well enjoy the lull while it lasted.

Judging by the sound of it, her peaceful, quiet life was about to come to an abrupt end.

CHAPTER EIGHT

JOSH'S mother had been quite right. The next day was Monday, and Fran had hoped he wouldn't do too much.

Josh plotted and planned instead, hobbling into his study and sitting at his desk until she had to nag him about having his leg down for too long.

Then he just decamped into the kitchen, taking over the sofa and coffee-table again, so that the beautiful flowers had to remove themselves to the breakfast table and her painting was ousted.

'Bang a nail in the wall,' Josh suggested, but she just looked at him, scandalised.

'I can't do that! It'll make a mark on the wall.'

He shrugged. 'So? It's my wall. Anyway, there's a gap there. I've been meaning to get something, although I suppose hanging in the kitchen wouldn't really be very good for it. You could put it in your bedroom, perhaps.'

She could, but she was rather hoping she wouldn't spend very much time in her bedroom any longer. She seemed to have moved into his, for the last night at least, but it was an idea. There certainly wasn't any room in the hall or the sitting room, he never ever seemed to use the dining-room, and the rest of the house was just guest accommodation really, apart from the library, and the walls in there were totally lined with books.

She went into her bedroom, and found a picture on the wall that she was much less fond of. It was a pastel drawing, behind glass, and much less likely to be damaged than her oil painting on canvas. She put the pastel into her wardrobe, hung Annie's much bigger painting in its place and stood back with a nod of satisfaction. There. She could always come in here and look at it.

Fran went back into the kitchen and perched on the end of the sofa.

'You need a break,' she told Josh.

'Hmm?' he mumbled, not really paying any attention to her at all, so she took the piece of paper out of his hand. That got his attention. 'Now what?' he said a trifle impatiently.

'I said, you need a break. I've put the coffee on— have a little walk round, stretch your legs.'

Josh gave her a jaundiced look. 'First of all it's "You're standing too much", now it's "Have a little walk round, stretch your legs". I wish you'd make your mind up.'

'You just need a healthy balance,' she pointed out, and he snorted.

'You sound like a supermarket slogan.'

'And you sound like an old grump,' she retorted. 'Come on, it's a lovely day, let's have a stroll outside.'

With an exaggerated sigh, he shuffled all the papers together and put them on the floor beside the sofa, then swung his legs down and stood up. 'Nag, nag,

nag, nag,' he muttered under his breath. 'And to think I pay you for that.'

Fran felt a twinge of hurt at that, but ignored it. She wished he hadn't brought the subject up, because she'd actually allowed herself to forget that she was supposed to be just doing a job. 'I'd hate you to think you weren't getting value for money,' she quipped with as much lightness as she could muster, and handed him the crutch. 'Come on, it'll do you good.'

They went slowly down the hall and out of the front door, and once he'd negotiated the step, he stood on the path and breathed in the wonderfully fresh air and sighed contentedly. 'It is gorgeous here,' he said quietly. 'I keep forgetting how lucky I am.'

They strolled over the grass towards the river. The house didn't really have a garden, just lawns around it that ran down towards the Deben, and the backdrop of trees behind it. Close to the house there were a few architectural plants set in big stones, but other than that the landscape had been left natural. It was very effective, because it didn't distract from the surroundings which still took her breath away every time she stopped to look at them.

As they walked, Josh talked about the exhibition.

'I think Annie's stuff will be very good, and there's another guy I've got lined up. We need to go and see him. He's quite different, much more abstract. He does a lot of work in pastels. In fact, he did the one in your room.'

She felt a pang of guilt, and confessed. 'Oops. I just took it down and put it in the wardrobe, so I could put Annie's picture up. I'm sorry.'

'Don't be. Annie's picture is much better. That was a very early one of his, and he's come on enormously. His stuff's really very lively now, full of energy. It's more like Annie's, but very different. I think the two styles will complement each other, but we'll see.'

Fran was relieved that Josh didn't seem to mind about the picture. Anyway, it was as much for the protection of Annie's picture as anything, so she didn't really see a problem.

'Can you explain something to me?' she said, wondering if he'd tell her to mind her own business. 'It's probably a stupid question, but what is it exactly that you do?'

'For a living?' He shrugged. 'I suppose I move money round, really. I buy and sell things—stocks and shares, property, companies—anything, really, that I think is going to improve. I started by accident. My father gave me some money for my eighteenth birthday, and I invested it. It did rather well, to everybody's amazement, and so I did it again, and then again. By that time, I had enough to buy a small terraced house, so I did. That's the one that Annie's living in. It didn't look like that then, but it was a house, and it was my first, and I was only twenty. I've kept it out of sentiment, renting it out, and Annie's lived in it for two years now. That's how I met her.'

He shot her a smile. 'Anyway, that was the start, really,' he told her. 'It just went on from there. I bought a small company, a huge speculative gamble that had my family in hysterics, but it paid off, and I turned it around and trebled its value in six months.

So that was that. I did it again, and again, and some-where along the line I ended up doing rather well.'

His grin was wry, and she thought it was wonderful that he hadn't got smug or arrogant about his talents.

'Doesn't it worry you when you have to make peo-ple redundant when you take over these companies?' she asked, wondering how that sat with him. 'You always hear of it happening.'

Josh nodded slowly. 'Oh, yes. I try and make sure that I don't hurt people, but I can't tolerate ineffi-ciency so every now and then someone has to go. Mostly, though, people just can't see what they're do-ing wrong, and with a little organisation and manage-ment they can make huge improvements. Often they're too close, they can't get far enough back to see the big picture. That's always much easier, com-ing in from the outside.'

Fran considered that for a moment, then tipped her head on one side. 'I suppose this makes you an en-trepreneur?' Fran suggested, but he pulled a face.

'I hate that word,' he said with a twisted little smile, 'it always sounds so tacky. It makes me sound like an asset stripper, and I like to think I'm a bit more scrupulous than that.'

She thought for a moment, and nodded. 'So, how do you see yourself? A bit of a modern-day Robin Hood, perhaps?'

Josh laughed. 'I don't know about that. I'm not that magnanimous. I know I live in the woods, but I hardly rough it, and anyway, I look ridiculous in tights.'

She pursed her lips thoughtfully, trying not to laugh

with him. 'I don't know. You might look sort of cute, but the fixator might be a bit of a problem.'

They strolled on towards the edge of the grass, and she turned and looked back over the forest behind them. 'You are lucky, though,' she said, going back to his original statement. 'Very few people are privileged enough to live in a beautiful place like this. It's not just the house, it's the whole setting that makes it so special.'

'Oh, absolutely. The house is just somewhere to live, somewhere to house my art collection. It's the view from the house that it's all about. If you notice, there are hardly any windows on the other side.'

She had noticed, and she thought it was a shame in a way because the woods were beautiful, too. She'd seen deer grazing on the edge of the woodland, and rabbits and foxes. It would be a wonderful place, she thought wistfully, to bring up children, and wondered again why he was so adamant that he wouldn't have any.

Well, he'd said grandchildren, but that was probably only because *she* had, and as far as she knew there were no inherited diseases that would predict the sterility of your own children and guarantee it in every case. So, he must have meant any children at all, and she thought that was desperately sad. He would make a wonderful father, she thought. She could picture him in the woods with a little boy with dark, sticky-up hair and bright blue eyes.

He stopped walking and turned her with a smile. 'Well, that's me. Tell me about you. Tell me about your nursing. You must have loved it once.'

She nodded. She had loved it, of course she had, and somehow, out here in the sunshine with him, she could talk about it.

'I trained in London,' she told him, going back to the beginning. 'It was easy for me, because my parents lived just outside Woodbridge and I could easily get home, so I didn't feel too homesick. Sometimes it was a lot of fun, sometimes I hated it, but on balance it was OK, and I always loved the nursing.'

'What attracted you to A and E?' he asked her.

'I don't know, really. It was just one of those odd things. They were very short-staffed, and I was asked if I could cover a shift. I said I would, and it was brilliant. I did it again a couple more times, and then I was hooked. A job came up, and I transferred and trained as a specialist trauma nurse and that was that. The next thing I knew, I was working full time on the trauma team, and I became an adrenalin junkie. The busier, the bloodier, the better.'

She fell silent, remembering the buzz of saving lives, the huge high when they stabilised an impossible case and sent them off to Theatre.

'So what happened?' Josh prompted softly. 'You seemed fine when I saw you in there—stressed, perhaps, but you seemed to enjoy it. So what went wrong?'

'It all started to go wrong. We had a run of disasters, lives that were never going to be saved—you know how it is, like buses, they all came at once. Day after day I would go to work, and people would bleed to death on me and I would have to go and try and explain to their relatives. How can you explain that?

How can you make any sense of it for someone, when there isn't any sense to be made? It's not possible, and I just couldn't do it any more. I fell apart one day at work just after you'd come in, and my boss sent me home.'

'For good?'

Fran shook her head. 'Not then. The next day was just as bad, and the day after that, and then he told me to leave. I suppose I was on the verge of a nervous breakdown, although I didn't realise it. They owed me three weeks' holiday, and they gave me the last week gratis, so I just stopped. They told me to go away and sort myself out, have a complete break, and when I feel better, they said, they'll have me back.'

'And do you?'

She shook her head again. 'No. That was three weeks ago now, and the further I get from it, the more I realise I don't want to go back ever. It was a part of my life that's over now, and I need to move on, but I just don't know where to.'

For a while Josh was silent, and she stared out over the water and felt the despair creep up on her again. Then he spoke again.

'So, what's the story of the boyfriend and flatmate?' he asked, probing gently.

She sighed, pausing beside a tree on the edge of the lawn and leaning back against it, turning her face up to the lovely autumn sunshine.

'He wasn't a serious boyfriend,' she explained. 'We weren't having an affair, but we were probably moving in that direction. Obviously not fast enough for him, though, because he clearly couldn't wait. I'd gone out "shopping", wandering aimlessly around Regent's Park crying my eyes out, wondering what on earth I was going to do with the rest of my life, and when I was exhausted I went back into Camden Town and had a cup of tea in a café.

'Then on my way back to the flat, somebody was knocked down right in front of me, and I just couldn't do anything. I froze, and somebody else took over and saved his life. Thank God they were there, because if they hadn't been, he would have died and I would have that on my conscience. Anyway, by the time I got home Dan had given up waiting for me and had moved in on Stella. I caught them, as they say, "*in flagrante*", so I just packed my clothes, picked up my books and my portable TV and my wash things, and I left.'

She remembered the awfulness of it, the dreadful emptiness. Homeless, jobless—it had been the lowest moment of her life, and she had been terrified.

'I didn't really know where to go. My parents have moved to Devon to be near my brother and sister-in-law, and none of them have any spare room, so I drove up to Woodbridge that night, stayed with Jackie and went into work with her in the morning. She didn't have anywhere really to put me up and, besides, I needed a job. She thought she'd be able to find me something residential and I'd had an interview with Xavier Giraud already. I was going to see him again that morning.'

'And then I walked in.'

Fran opened her eyes and turned her head to face

him. 'Yes,' she said softly, 'then you walked in, and things started to get a lot, lot better.'

Josh put his arm round her shoulders and hugged her affectionately. She rested her head on his shoulder and waited, but he didn't say anything, at least not about that. Still, what was he supposed to say—Things got better for me, too. I love you, you've changed my life? Hardly. Not even she was that blindly optimistic.

After a moment he lifted his head. 'Did you say something about coffee earlier?' he said, and she nodded, crushing her foolish disappointment.

'I've put it on, it should be ready for us now.'

They strolled back up the lawn, or at least she strolled, and he limped awkwardly and struggled with the slightly uneven ground. Then they were back inside on the oak floor, and it was easier. While he settled himself down on the sofa again, she poured the coffee and rummaged in the cupboard for a packet of chocolate biscuits.

'So, what are we going to do for the rest of the day?' she asked him, settling down cross-legged at the end of the sofa.

He arched an eyebrow. 'We? Well, I don't know what you're doing, but I've got to sort through this lot and then make a few phone calls. Why? Did you want to go somewhere? You don't have to stay here with me, you know. Isn't it time you had a day off?'

Day off? Why did she need a day off—except, of course, that it was just a job, and she was just an employee? She sighed soundlessly and dunked a biscuit in her coffee. 'I don't need a day off,' she said. 'I've just had three days of playing in London, and yesterday was wonderful. Why on earth would I need another day off?'

He lowered his coffee-mug, resting it on his belt buckle and looked at her thoughtfully. 'So what do you want to do?'

She shrugged. 'Isn't there anything I can do to help you with this lot?'

'If you really want to. It's all in a bit of a muddle, and I can't really stretch far enough to sort it out. That would be very useful, actually.'

So when they'd finished their coffee, she got down on her hands and knees on the floor beside him and shuffled papers while he directed her and told her which piles to put them on.

Fran found it quite interesting. Between what he'd said that morning and what she could glean from the pieces of paper, she was able to put together a clearer picture of what it was Josh really did.

He was in the middle of negotiating for a company, apparently, a small engineering firm in Suffolk that made components for garage doors. They'd developed a new hinge system that was smoother and more reliable, and also lighter to operate, but they didn't have the marketing or production know-how to get it off the ground. Josh was going to give them that chance, in exchange for a share in the profits.

'What happens if it doesn't work?' Fran asked him, but he just shrugged.

'Swings and roundabouts, really. You win some, you lose some. It's only money. It's happened before, no doubt it'll happen again.'

And with that string of clichés, he buried his nose back in the pile of papers on his lap and left her to it for a minute.

Only money, Fran thought, and wondered what it was like to have the luxury of being able to think that.

Odd, she decided, and carried on shuffling his papers.

For the next few days, Josh would open his post and make a few phone calls, then after lunch he would have a short rest before they visited the gallery to check on the progress of the building work.

Their days developed a kind of rhythm, a steady routine that seemed to suit his poor, battered body. Every few days he had to go to the hospital for a check-up at the fracture clinic, and Fran found it difficult every time. Still, now she was sharing his bed the nightmare didn't seem to trouble her as often, or as deeply.

Their relationship settled into a familiar and comfortable routine, along with the pattern of their days. They would shower together, sometimes quickly, sometimes much, much more slowly, and in the evenings they would sprawl together on the sofa in the kitchen and watch television or listen to music while they sipped their way gradually through the contents of his wine cellar.

Fran learnt the difference between the grapes, and the effect that altitude or temperature or rainfall could have on them, and he told her that even in the same vineyard, slopes with a different orientation to the sun could produce quite different wines.

He made the torturous journey down the stairs from the kitchen to the wine cellar again, muttering something about installing a stairlift, and then, one by one, he pulled bottles from the rack and told her the story of the vineyard, the lives of the families. He seemed to know them all personally, and she realised that he had actually invested in several of them. Did he, she wondered, take his profit in kind?

Unlikely. For all he was so interested in the wines, he rarely drank more than two glasses, and he savoured every mouthful.

And then after their wine-tasting session they would go to bed, in his huge, wide bed in that lovely bedroom, and he would take her in his arms and make love to her tenderly, carefully but very, very thoroughly. Sometimes he was too tired, but then he would wake in the night and turn to her, and for her that was even more magical.

There was something infinitely precious about these times they had together, and she stored them all away like a mental video that she could run in a later time, when this was all over.

Because it would be over, she knew that, just as she knew the sun would rise in the east. It would be over, and she would be alone as she had never been alone before.

Some idiot had once said it was better to have loved and lost than never to have loved at all. She wasn't sure, but just in case it was true and she wanted to wallow in memories, she filed them all carefully away in a little box marked JOSH. HANDLE WITH CARE.

October turned into November, and Josh had his cast removed from his arm in the second week.

'Bliss,' he said, and scratched it furiously all the way home.

'You'll make the skin sore,' she chided, trying to stop him, but he didn't care. He'd been sticking pens and chopsticks and anything else he could find down there for ages to try and scratch it, and he wasn't stopping for anyone.

'I want a shower,' he told her as she pulled up on the drive, 'without that damn bin bag. I want to wash my arm, and move it, and generally feel free again. I want to clean my teeth with it. And I want to touch you.'

She coloured softly, as she so often did, and he wondered how on earth she'd managed as a nurse with the male patients teasing her.

'What are we waiting for, then?' she asked, and he got out of the car and walked carefully up the steps and in the front door.

'Last one there's a sissy,' he said, knowing quite well that she'd easily beat him, but she just laughed and said it was no fun on her own, and she undressed him and stripped off her own clothes and turned on the shower.

They didn't get up again that day, and Josh tried hard not to think about Fran and what she was coming to mean to him. He was starting to rely on her, not only for physical help with getting around and all his daily personal tasks but for company and entertainment and companionship.

That was something he'd never wanted before. He'd always been rather solitary, and his women had been decorative and funny and they'd played by the rules.

Fran didn't. She sneaked under his guard time and time again, and he realised with something close to horror that he was falling for her.

It scared him spitless.

CHAPTER NINE

ALL work on the gallery was completed by the last week in November, due in no small part, Fran was sure, to Josh's constant nagging and bullying. Angus had finally handed the keys over to Josh and left the site, and all that remained to do was to prepare the exhibition.

All! Josh stood in the middle of the main exhibition room and stared around at the empty space.

'Well, he did it,' he said quietly. 'I did wonder if he would.'

'Probably not, if you hadn't kept on at him.'

He smiled at her tiredly. 'I think you're right. Still, it's done. The coffee-shop people are coming in to-morrow and setting up, and the van's coming with all the artwork the day after. At least now we can get the heating on and start warming this place up. It's freezing. I wonder if all the radiators work?'

'There's nothing more you can do here today,' she said gently. 'Come home now. Have an early night. You've got a long day tomorrow, if I know you. You'll want to supervise all of it.'

His grin was crooked. 'How well you know me,' he murmured. 'OK. Let's go home. Let's pick up a

take-away on the way, so you don't have to cook.
You look bushed. You've been working too hard.'

He reached out and brushed the back of his hand
over her cheek, and smiled gently. 'Thank you for all
your help with this, you've been a star.'

'My pleasure.'

Josh looked exhausted, and Fran was worried about
him, but as his mother had suggested she'd been
working alongside him and taking as much of the load
off him as possible. She couldn't have done more, so
her conscience at least was clear.

They'd been to see Joe, the young Irishman with
the pastels, and Fran thought he couldn't have been
more different to Annie.

Where she was small, he was tall and gangling,
where she was bright and outgoing he was dour and
sullen, and, unlike Annie, he'd completely ignored
Fran. He'd talked to Josh, his hand movements busy
and urgent, intense, and Fran had thought, Heavens,
here's a young man who takes himself far too seri-
ously.

His work, though, she had to admit, had come on
enormously from the pastel that had hung in her bedroom. His current work was much bolder, great
slashes of colour over the paper, and although she still
didn't like them as much as Annie's, the styles com-
plemented each other and in a curious way his drawings set off her figures, making them seem less bi-
zarre.

She was looking forward to seeing it all assembled,

she thought—if they all lived that long. She was more tired than she'd been in ages, more tired than coming off duty in A and E, or after her first set of night shifts.

They went home and ate their take-away half-heartedly, then fell into bed and slept right through till the morning. For almost the first time they didn't make love, and in the morning Josh was unusually reluctant to get out of bed.

He was exhausted still, she realised, and she wondered if she should pull rank and tell him to rest, but she knew it was a waste of time. He'd insist on supervising—but she could at least make him sit down, and if the coffee-shop people were coming in, maybe they would have coffee and tea and other refreshments on site so she could make him take regular breaks.

It took the whole day to install all the partitions that would divide up the space, and then a professional team, despatched by Josh, collected all the artwork from Annie and Joe and delivered it to the gallery the following day.

That was when the real work began in earnest, and Josh started overdoing it, walking without his crutch, carrying things with his right arm and generally stressing his abdominal incisions before the muscles were properly healed.

Fran forced tea and coffee down him at hideously regular intervals, and in between she kept parking him on a chair and making him sit to look at the evolving display. He wouldn't sit, though, and said it was important to be at eye level.

'So pretend you're short,' she snapped, and he just raised a brow and carried on, ignoring her.

It took ages to hang them all, and Fran was up to her neck in it. There was obviously going to be no way she could drag Josh away from it, and the only thing she found that worked was attaching herself to him like a shadow and doing for him everything he tried to do.

Then Annie's birthday present to her and the sculptures from Josh's sitting room were delivered, and everything was thrown into a state of flux again.

Finally, after two days of shuffling and rearranging, all the works were displayed to everybody's satisfaction, and a catalogue could be prepared.

Josh had engaged a woman from a secretarial agency to do it for them, and Fran finally persuaded him to leave her with Annie and Joe to number them all and prepare the list, ready for typing. He was out on his feet, his skin a terrible colour, dark circles round his eyes and lines of pain bracketing his mouth, and she really wasn't happy with him.

'You've done too much,' she chided gently. 'I should have stopped you.'

He dropped his head back against the headrest and rolled it towards her with a sigh. 'Nobody could have stopped me,' he assured her. 'It had to be done—now it is. I can rest now.'

'Too right you can rest,' she muttered. 'You're going right home to bed, and you aren't going to the gallery before midday tomorrow—'

'You're bossy.'

'You're stupid. You need to rest.'

'I will rest. I'll rest tonight,' he promised, but when she got him home he looked worse, and she put him to bed and called the doctor.

Dr Giraud was still at the surgery, and he promised to come on his way home.

'I won't be long—a few minutes, that's all,' he promised. 'Give me the directions, would you? I don't think I've ever visited him.'

So she told him the way, and went back to Josh. 'Can I get you anything?' she asked, but he shook his head.

'No, I feel sick. I'll just go to sleep.'

Her heart started racing. Nausea, pallor, exhaustion—all signs of a slow internal bleed, perhaps an aortic aneurysm that hadn't been diagnosed, or a gently leaking spleen that was about to burst through the encapsulating membrane...

'You're crazy,' she told herself sternly. 'He's fine.'

But she stood in his bedroom, peering through the window that overlooked the drive and waiting for the doctor's car, and while she waited she prayed that he wouldn't bleed to death like everyone in her dreams.

A few minutes later she caught sight of the approaching headlights in the blackness of the winter night, and went quickly to the door and let Dr Giraud in.

'He's been overdoing it,' she said. 'He's been con-
verting a warehouse on the quay to a gallery, and
we've been putting all the stuff in for the first exhibition for the past two days. I just couldn't get him
to stop.'

Dr Giraud nodded and gave her an understanding
smile. 'Men can be very stubborn,' he said. 'Young,
usually fit men are often the worst. Don't worry, I'll
have a good look at him. What do you feel is wrong?'

Fran shrugged. 'I don't know. I'm overreacting, but
I keep thinking he's haemorrhaging.' She ran through
the symptoms, and Giraud nodded.

'OK, it's unlikely he's haemorrhaging—after all
this time. I don't think so. How are the pins in his
fixator, or is it off yet? He might just have a pin track
infection. They can be quite difficult to see, especially
with all the stuff in the way. Has he got an elevated
temperature?'

Fran stared at him in amazement. Of course! That
was all that was wrong with him, a simple pin track
infection. Nasty enough, but not a patch on her other
diagnosis. She felt her shoulders slump.

'I don't know. I didn't take it. I'd already decided
he was bleeding to death.' She shook her head. 'I'm
sorry, I'm not usually this vacant, but it's been busy.
So busy. I've been helping him, trying to slow him
down, and I haven't been concentrating on the nursing.'

'And just think,' he teased gently, 'you could have
been working for me and having a quiet life.'

She could—but then she wouldn't have had Josh, and she couldn't imagine life without him.

She showed Dr Giraud into the bedroom, and he chatted to Josh for a moment, quietly observing him, and then he turned back the covers and examined Josh's leg, and there on the front of his shin was a tiny red patch around the entry site of one of the pins.

What an idiot! How could she have missed it? She couldn't have been doing her job properly.

'I don't think it's anything to worry about,' he said. 'The bone seems to be knitting well, and I expect it'll be off soon, won't it?'

Josh nodded. 'He said another couple of weeks, then it'll go into a cast.'

'OK. I'll give you a prescription for antibiotics, and then you must drink plenty of fluids—no coffee, no tea, no alcohol—and you should be feeling much better in a day or two. But stay off it, at least for twenty-four to forty-eight hours—all right?'

Josh opened his mouth to protest, but Fran just smiled. 'That'll be fine. I'll make sure he stays in bed all day tomorrow and then uses the chair for the next couple of days, or at least until the exhibition opens on Friday night.'

Giraud's mouth kicked up in a smile, and Fran noticed for the first time just what an attractive man he was. He ought to smile more. How sad that he'd lost his wife and was alone, she thought. He probably didn't have very much to smile about.

He opened his bag and looked through it, then patted his pockets and sighed.

'I've run out of prescription forms,' he said heavily. 'I'm sorry. I've got more at home, but I can't leave my children. The lady who's covering for me in the afternoons is supposed to go at seven, and it's after that already, but he needs it tonight—I'll have to put the kids in the car and bring it to you.'

'Can I come to you and collect it?' Fran asked, and he shrugged.

'Well—sure, but I didn't want to put you out.'

'Don't worry,' Fran assured him. You aren't. I'd have to go into town to collect it, so it won't be far out of my way, and you don't want to drag the children out on a cold night. I don't suppose you live far away?'

'No—about ten minutes from here, that's all. Are you sure you don't mind?'

'Quite sure. It's no problem.'

'Give me five minutes, then, and I'll have it ready for you.'

He told her the way, and after she'd got Josh a drink and made him comfortable she went down via the kitchen stairs and took her car out of the garage. It was time she gave it a run, she thought, it had been sitting neglected for too long.

It seemed tiny—tiny and very vulnerable. No wonder Josh had felt insecure in it so soon after his crash, and no wonder he'd wanted something bigger. Maybe when her finances were a bit more secure she'd trade it in for something a bit more robust.

She followed Dr Giraud's instructions, chastising herself all the way for missing that infection, and then turned in through the gateposts he'd described, and faltered.

The house looks familiar, she thought, puzzled. How odd.

It was Georgian, with a door in the middle and windows each side, just like a child's drawing of a typical house, only a little grander.

Not too grand, not so grand it wasn't comfortable, by any means, but elegant and well proportioned.

And familiar. How odd, she thought again.

Fran rang the doorbell, and a voice called out, 'Come in.'

She did, opening the door cautiously, and stared at the black and white tiled floor.

I've dreamt about this house, she thought. He's going to come out of a room over there and kiss my hand—

'Miss Williams. I'm sorry about this. Thank you so much for coming over, it was very kind of you.'

Dr Giraud held out his hand to her, and she lifted hers, mesmerised. Heavens, she thought, he's going to kiss it.

'Here. The prescription. I hope he soon feels better. Give me a ring in the morning at the surgery if not, or if you're worried at all. I'm not on duty, we have a deputising service now, but feel free to ring me.

I've put the number on there just in case you should need it.'

She took the prescription and tucked it in her bag, wondering if she looked as foolish and shell-shocked as she felt.

'You look as if you could do with getting to bed yourself,' he said quietly. 'You look shattered. Has he been working you hard?'

Fran laughed softly. 'Not nursing him, not directly, but the only way to stop him doing too much is to take over what he's trying to do. The trouble is, he just goes and finds something else to do, and he's been running me ragged like that for days!'

He chuckled. 'Well, I hope the exhibition is a great success. Everyone's talking about it. I hope to go on Friday night—perhaps I'll see you there.'

She looked into his eyes, and again the feeling of *déjà vu* hit her. Lost eyes—sad, endlessly lonely eyes, she thought, and ached for him.

'Thank you for coming out to Josh,' she said, and shook his hand.

'My pleasure. I would offer you the job again, but I have a feeling you won't be needing one,' he said with a slow smile.

Fran just hoped he was right.

'How do I look?'

Fran stood back and eyed Josh critically. 'Not bad,' she said, a slow smile playing around her mouth. 'Not bad at all.' She studied the trousers, held together below the knee on the right leg with a tacking stitch. She'd let in an extra bit of black fabric to disguise the fixator, and had then tacked him into them once they were on. She decided now that if you didn't know, you probably wouldn't notice.

'I think you'll pass,' she said, giving it one last look, then she ran her eyes over the rest of him and her heart hiccuped. Goodness, she'd got so used to him in sloppy jeans and old jumpers that this immaculate man with the startlingly white shirt and black satin bow-tie was a total stranger.

A very sexy, very appealing stranger, who was looking at her with hungry eyes.

'You look wonderful,' he said in a low, slightly husky voice. 'Elegant and beautiful and good enough to eat. I'll have to save some room for later.'

The promise was hot in his eyes, and she felt her skin warm at their caress.

'You do that.'

She looked at herself in his long mirror. She was wearing a dress that she'd bought for the occasion, with a low scooped neckline and tiny spaghetti straps. It was black, just a short cocktail dress, but it was undeniably elegant and she had glossy sheer black tights on that made her legs look endless.

'Stay there,' Josh ordered softly, and he came up behind her and brushed a light, lingering kiss over her bare shoulders, his eyes on hers in the mirror.

'Close your eyes,' he told her. She felt him move closer, and then something cool brushed against her neck, settling in the hollow of her throat. Her lids fluttered, and he said, 'Uh-uh. Keep them shut.'

Jewellery, she thought. He's giving me jewellery. Oh, lord. What does it mean?

She could feel his fingers at the back of her neck, fiddling with the catch, and then he smoothed the chain and stepped away.

'OK, you can open your eyes now.'

She opened them and stared, her jaw sagging slightly. It was a diamond—at least, it looked like a diamond, although she'd never seen one that size— shaped like a teardrop, the setting very simple, with nothing to detract from the clear, brilliant light of the stone.

'Josh?' she whispered, and turned to him, her heart racing.

'It's just a thank you, for all you've done.'

A thank you? That sounded ominous. 'You don't need to thank me,' she said, panicking. Thank you and goodbye. Oh, please, no.

'Yes, I do. I wouldn't have got the gallery finished without you, and I certainly wouldn't have enjoyed it the way I have. I owe you a huge debt of gratitude.' His mouth kicked up in a rueful smile. 'I know I've given you a hard time for nagging me, but you needed to, or I probably wouldn't have been here at all, and I'm really grateful. So—thank you.'

He drew her into his arms and kissed her, just lightly, then lifted his head and looked down at her. 'You look absolutely beautiful tonight,' he said, his voice soft and utterly sincere, and Fran swallowed hard and smiled.

'Thank you,' she said, finally daring to accept his compliment, and her heart soared. Maybe it wasn't goodbye at all…

He cleared his throat and stepped back. 'Right. We ought to go. Are you ready?'

She nodded. 'I will be just as soon as I have my coat on.'

'OK. Let's hit the road.'

The night was a great success. Josh circulated, a smile on his face, busily networking on behalf of his artists, and by the end of the evening there were several little red dots scattered about the room.

Even a pair of Annie's tortured figures had sold, he thought in amazement, although in this setting, oddly enough, they looked really very good. Perhaps it was a question of scale and maybe his sitting room, for all its size, just wasn't big enough to do them justice.

In any event it was going well, and everyone seemed to be genuinely enjoying themselves. The wine was flowing freely, and so was the laughter, and there didn't seem to be anybody who needed his attention.

In which case, he thought, he'd find Fran. The last time he'd seen her she'd been deep in conversation with the doctor, and now she seemed to have disappeared.

He looked around again, and there she was, laughing with Annie over something someone had said. They seemed to be getting along fine, he thought, absently rubbing his thigh. It ached tonight, but at least the pin track infection seemed to have been knocked on the head.

How much of it had been the infection and how much sheer exhaustion, he didn't know, but he'd felt drained for two days and he'd been only too happy to let Fran bully him into staying in bed.

Still, the private view was a roaring success, the gallery was up and running with its coffee-shop and gift shop all ready to go, his take-over of the local engineering company was all sewn up and he could put his feet up now until after Christmas. In fact, he thought, he could do with putting his feet up now, but nobody seemed to be showing any signs of leaving.

Josh looked around, wondering how Joe was doing. He was a little awkward, not a people person like Annie, and he'd been dreading this view, but when Josh saw him he seemed much more relaxed. He was chatting up the daughter of one of Woodbridge's more notable citizens, and she was hanging on his every word.

Josh smiled slightly. Nothing like an adoring female to make you feel better, he thought, and wondered where Fran was now. She'd moved and he'd lost her.

He was about to turn round when he sensed her

behind him. She slipped her arms round his waist, resting her head briefly on his shoulder and giving him a quick, affectionate squeeze.

'Are you OK?' she asked softly.

He turned round and smiled at her. 'I'm fine. A bit tired. My leg aches a bit.'

'Do you need to stay to the end?'

He nodded. 'I do, really.'

She shrugged. 'I don't know. Catherine's going to be running the gallery, and she's here, and the two artists are here—I would have thought you could slide off. You've got a good excuse, after all.'

But he shook his head. There was something he needed to say to her—something very important—and he wanted his mind clear. He didn't want to be worrying about the private view and how it was going.

'We'll stay,' he said. It couldn't be much longer…

It was another hour before everyone had gone home, and by the time the car finally pulled up outside Josh's house, it was after midnight.

He had been on his feet all day, and Fran was worried about him, but he seemed fine. A little tired, a little sore, maybe a bit distracted, but nothing to worry about.

In fact, she thought, he really didn't need a nurse any more, and he hadn't for a while, if she was honest. He needed a chauffeur, he needed a housekeeper—well, really, he needed a wife, but that wouldn't happen. She was realistic enough to know that. Odd remarks he'd made over the weeks, little clues, all added up to a man who was terrified of commitment, and she guessed his parents were largely responsible. It would take a better woman than her to convince him.

The garage door slid quietly up, and she drove the car in and parked it beside hers, zapped the garage door remote again and then hopped out and went round to help Josh. He was there before her, though, shutting the car door as she reached him, and as he walked towards her his limp was almost unnoticeable.

He was almost there now, almost recovered. It had been nine weeks since his accident, and everything except his lower leg was well on the mend. That, too, would be sorted in the next month or so probably, and then he'd be able to drive again.

And then, Fran told herself, he really won't need you any more, you or anyone.

Her hand went to her throat subconsciously, as it had all evening, and she felt the diamond teardrop with fingertips that tingled with fear. It was coming to an end, she thought. Would he still want her?

They went upstairs, his progress slow but much better than before, and she followed him up, her heart filled with dread.

'Do you want a coffee?' she said brightly as they crossed the kitchen, but he shook his head.

'No. Come here. I want to talk to you. There's something I need to say.'

Oh, lord. Her heart pounding, her mouth dry, she went over to him and perched beside him on the sofa.

He took her hand, rubbing her fingers absently with his thumb, staring down at the floor.

'This is very difficult,' he said gruffly. 'I don't really know where to begin.'

Josh took a steadying breath, then went on, 'I really meant it when I said how grateful I was for all your help. I don't know how I would have coped without you for the past few weeks. You've been wonderful to me, and I really would have struggled without you.'

His fingers tightened on her hand, but she didn't respond. Here we go, she thought. Just say it.

'The fact is,' he said slowly, 'I've been thinking for the past few days that I really don't need a nurse any more. I need someone to drive me around for a while, but apart from that I can cope now.'

Fran's heart slowed right down, then crashed against her ribs. Well, she'd known it was coming.

She gently eased her hand away and stood up, crossing to the window. 'I know. I've been thinking that, too,' she said, her voice surprisingly steady. She was proud of herself for that. Dignity, after all, was all she had left.

'Actually, I have another job to go to. I was talking to Dr Giraud tonight. They still need a practice nurse. I've been thinking I might do that. It's not front line, but I don't want that any more, so it would be ideal, and in the meantime Jackie has something lined up for me, another residential post. A lady's waiting to come out of hospital. She just needs home cover for a week or two. So don't worry about me, I'm sorted. In fact, I can start with her tomorrow.'

There was silence for a moment, then he said quietly, 'And is that what you want? To do that?'

She nodded, blinking back the stupid tears that were threatening to fall.

'Yes. Yes, I think so. I'll see. Perhaps I'll have some time off and go and see my parents.' She turned, smiling brightly. 'So that's that sorted. You don't need to worry about me, and I don't need to worry about you.'

Her hands went up to the necklace, and the catch yielded to her touch. 'Here,' she said, holding it out to him. 'It's lovely, but it's far too much. I can't possibly keep it. I enjoyed wearing it, though.'

He didn't move, so she put it on the coffee-table in front of him, and he just stared at it.

She went into her room, hanging on by a thread, and pulled out her case. She only had a few clothes, and she packed swiftly, gathering all her other things and putting them together on the bed.

There were just her wash things to collect from Josh's bathroom, and she was done. She went into his room and stared at the bed, rumpled from them sitting on it as they'd dressed for the evening, and remembered the beautiful, tender love they'd shared.

Don't think about it. Just don't think about it, she told herself fiercely, and quickly gathered up her things. She threw them in her case, zipped it shut and scooped up all the other bags and bits.

He was still sitting there, the diamond dangling from his fingers now, light sparkling from it as it revolved slowly on the chain.

'Goodbye, Josh,' she said. 'Thank you for everything.'

He looked up, his face shuttered and withdrawn.

'You're leaving?' he said, his voice harsh, and she nodded.

'I think it's best, don't you?' She swallowed hard. 'Take care of yourself.'

And then she turned and walked slowly and calmly down the stairs and out of his life.

She'd left the garage door open, Josh realised numbly. He stood on the balcony of his bedroom, watching her car's tail-lights disappear down the track, and his heart felt cold and empty.

Fran had gone, every trace of her removed.

Well, almost every trace. He looked down at the diamond winking in his hand, and hurled it away towards the river. It arced through the air, sparkled once and fell soundlessly to the ground.

His hand dropped to his side. It was for the best, he told himself. Letting himself get so close to her had been a mistake. It was as well she was gone—a clean cut, precise, like a surgeon's blade.

So why did it feel as if his heart had been torn out?

CHAPTER TEN

FRAN made it to the end of the track, then collapsed over the steering-wheel, unable to breathe for the huge, racking sobs that were tearing through her body.

She thought she was going to die, thought the pain of it would kill her, and then after an age she realised that it wouldn't be that easy. She wasn't going to die. She was going to live, but alone, without Josh, for years and years and years...

The sobs started again, ripping through her mercilessly, and she had no choice but to let the storm of weeping subside. Then she blew her nose, scrubbed at her swollen eyes and straightened her shoulders.

She'd cope. She was a fighter. Worse things had happened to her.

Surely?

She tried to think of anything worse, anything she'd gone through and survived, and the only thing that came to mind was losing her job because she'd fallen apart.

And Josh had put her back together again, holding her, loving her, rebuilding her confidence—or so she'd thought, until tonight.

Her eyes filled again, and she blinked fiercely and

sniffed. No. She wouldn't start all that again. She was going to put him behind her, forget him.

She turned the engine on again and drove up the road, then hesitated at the traffic lights. Left or right? Left was into town, right was towards the country.

Towards Xavier.

She shook her head. He didn't want to see her, not at this time of night, and looking as she did she wasn't at all sure she wanted to see him. She didn't even know why she was thinking about him, except that she'd seen him earlier and had thought again what kind, caring eyes he had.

He'd be kind to her now, but she probably didn't need that at the moment, not if she wasn't going to fall apart again. Besides, he had enough problems of his own without her adding to them.

Fran turned left, towards Woodbridge and Jackie, and ten minutes later she was curled up in her friend's sitting room, pouring her heart out and being offered tea and sympathy. It didn't take away the pain, but it did make her feel better.

Not enough, though, and she woke in the night to the sound of someone sobbing and realised it was her.

'I don't think you're fit to work at the moment,' Jackie told her firmly. 'You can't go and sit with someone who is ill for hour after hour, with nothing to occupy your mind, and not just sink into self-pity.'

'So give me something busy to do,' Fran begged her, but Jackie shook her head.

'I haven't got anything—not busy enough. The only thing busy enough would be A and E, and I haven't got any call for that through my agency. And besides, you really aren't fit for that.'

No, Fran thought numbly. She wasn't. She wasn't fit for anything, Jackie was right, and so she packed all her things up again into the boot of her car and drove down to Devon to see her parents.

They took one look at her and drew her into the safe, caring embrace of their home, and for the next two weeks she walked miles over the cliffs and up on Dartmoor, and visited her brother and sister-in-law and played with the children and tried not to cry in front of any of them.

She lost weight, her face grew thin and drawn, and her clothes hung on her. Her mother tried to feed her up but she couldn't eat, the sofa was too short so she couldn't sleep, she couldn't concentrate on anything and she just wanted to cry the entire time.

Then finally she decided to take herself in hand and sort her life out. She couldn't go on like this any more. Xavier Giraud had a job for her, and she needed to go back up to Suffolk, find herself a flat and get on with her life. She felt lost down here, so far from everything she'd ever known, and stupidly she felt too far from Josh.

She needed to be nearer to him, needed to be able to walk along the riverbank and see his house on the opposite shore high up above the water, and go to his gallery and see the exhibitions.

She had to pick her painting up at some time, too, and it wouldn't hurt to have a wall to hang it on, she thought.

And so she went back, in the last week in December, with Christmas thankfully over and a new year ahead. The first thing she did was contact Jackie, and then she found herself a little flat on a short lease, rang Xavier about the job and arranged to start at the beginning of January.

So far, so good. All she had to do now was see about picking up her painting when the exhibition closed because that she really did want to keep.

It was the longest month of Josh's life. He'd thought he'd hit rock bottom when he'd had his accident. Now he knew he hadn't even scratched the surface.

Everywhere he went, Fran was there. He could picture her so easily, her quick smile, her wide grey eyes soft with loving or flashing sparks of temper when he'd upset her.

No wonder she'd gone, he thought. Obviously it had meant less to her than it had to him, but he'd always known it was a temporary thing. It always was, with women. They didn't have what it took to stay the course. Look at his mother.

Still, at least Fran had gone before he'd said too much, so his pride was intact.

Not that it did him any good. His pride was a cold bedfellow, and he missed her like he'd never imagined he could miss anyone before. Josh stared out over the river and swallowed hard. He was so lonely here now. He'd never been lonely before, just alone.

That was fine. He liked being alone, he was naturally a bit of a loner.

Or he had been, until Fran. Now he was just restless and empty, and nothing could hold his attention for long.

He heard a car coming, and leant towards the window to see who was visiting him. He caught a flash of red and his heart sank.

His mother.

Oh, damn. She'd lecture him about eating, complain that he hadn't answered her calls and ask him if he'd heard from Fran.

He really, really didn't need to see her, but it was too late. She'd walked up the path and waved at him, and she would expect to be let in. With a sigh he stood up and limped slowly to the door and opened it, and she breezed in.

'I was just passing and I thought I'd drop in and see you, since you never bother to ring me back or answer my messages. Hello, darling.' She stretched up and held out her cheek, and Josh bent and kissed it dutifully.

'Hello, Mother,' he said expressionlessly. 'How are you?'

'Oh, I'm fine. I've been at the sales. I've bought Roger some things, and there was a lovely jumper I just had to have. I've brought you some fruit and some vitamins from that wonderful health shop—oh, and I saw Fran.'

His heart stopped, then crashed against his ribs. 'Fran?' he croaked, following her up the hall.

'Yes. She looked dreadful—thin and pale. I don't think she's looking after herself. In fact,' she said, turning and eyeing him up and down, 'she looks a lot like you.'

She went into the kitchen and put the kettle on, then fiddled about washing the teapot and finding tea bags, clattering mugs and looking for the milk until he was ready to scream.

'Where did you see her?' he asked, leaning against the breakfast bar because his legs had suddenly turned to jelly and wouldn't support him.

'In the Thoroughfare. She didn't see me. She was staring in a shop window.' She stopped fiddling and turned towards him. 'She looked miserable, Josh.'

He shrugged and turned away. 'It was her choice to leave.'

'Well, I think she's regretting it.'

He snorted. 'Tough. What am I supposed to do, go after her and beg her to change her mind?'

He would have done, over and over again in the past few weeks, if he'd had any slight idea where she was, but his mother didn't know that and he wasn't even happy admitting it to himself.

'You could,' she said, coming over to the sofa and putting down two mugs of tea on the coffee-table. 'Biscuit?'

'No, I don't want a bloody biscuit,' he snapped, ramming his hand through his hair. His leg was aching, and he wanted to hit something. He eyed the wall thoughtfully, then considered his broken wrist and sat down with a sigh.

'I'm sorry,' he said heavily. 'I'm just a bit raw at the moment.'

'I know.' She put a hand on his knee and squeezed it gently, then retreated to her tea. 'I do understand, Josh. I know just what it's like to love someone when you can't be with them.'

'I don't love her,' he said flatly.

'Oh, I think you do. I think you love her very much. Why else are you turning yourself inside out?'

'Well, it's pointless anyway. She'll only leave me in the end, just like you left my father. That's what women do, isn't it? Leave? It's better now than later.'

She stared at him for a moment, then sighed, as if she'd made a decision. 'Your father left me first, Josh.'

He stared at her in astonishment. 'No. No, he didn't, you left him! I remember it.'

'No. He left me, over and over again for years. I went through hell with your father, and every time he left me for another woman, I said it was the last time, but I always had him back. And then I met Roger, the summer you were fourteen, and I realised what it was like to be truly loved. So I left your father, and you stayed with him because he told you what a wicked woman I was.'

Her eyes filled with tears. 'I lost you at that moment, and I've never got you back. I grieved for you so much.'

Josh opened his mouth to say something, then shut it again. 'He'd had affairs?' he said eventually, slowly sorting it all out in his mind.

'Oh, yes. Dozens of them. He had endless women trailing after him. He was like you, rich and good-looking. Women wanted him, and why should he say no? He didn't really love me any more, if he ever had, and I only stayed with him for you. Then you were fourteen and I had a chance of happiness with Roger, and I took it.'

'Why didn't you tell me he was a liar?' he asked her, but she just shook her head slowly.

'And destroy him in your eyes? He was your hero, Josh. I was just your mother. I didn't realise I was going to lose you, and by the time I did, it was too late. The damage was done.'

He stared at the floor between his feet, remembering all the rows in his childhood, snatches of arguments overheard by a small boy sitting at the top of the stairs, fear in his heart.

If it wasn't for the child, I'd leave you for good!
If it wasn't for Joshua, I wouldn't be here!

'I'm sorry,' he said gruffly. 'I seem to have done you rather an injustice.'

'Not you, darling. It wasn't your fault.'

'So why tell me now, after all these years?'

'Because of Fran,' she said simply. 'Because you

love her, and something's getting in the way. You're
afraid to trust, but you don't need to be. You're like
me, not like your father, when it comes to relation-
ships. You've got what it takes to stay, to hang on
and sort out the problems. Your father never did, but,
then, he only ever thought about himself. You were
never like that. You were the most generous and
thoughtful child I'd ever met, and you've grown up
into a considerate and generous adult. You deserve to
be happy, and I think you were happy with Fran.'

'I thought you hated her?'

'Fran? No. I was just jealous. I wanted to look after
you, to care for you in a way I'd been denied for so
many years, but she got here first. And as I got to
know her, I didn't hate her at all. I thought she was
lovely, and strong enough to stand up to you. You
need that. Someone you can respect.'

Josh swallowed hard, but the lump in his throat just
stayed there. He picked up his tea and took a gulp,
burning his mouth, but he didn't care. He didn't care
about anything any more.

Only Fran.

He sipped his tea again, more cautiously, and tried
to picture her thin and pale, and failed miserably.
She'd never been fat, but she'd been womanly, soft
and smooth and rounded, and her cheeks were usually
flushed with health or temper or arousal, not pale.

So she was still in Woodbridge. He wondered if
Jackie had known that all along and had lied to him,
or if Fran had been away and come back. Whatever,

she was here now, and the nursing agency was just near the quay.

He put his tea down and turned to his mother.

'Can you give me a lift into town? I need to go to the gallery. I can get a taxi back.'

She studied him thoughtfully for a moment, then put down her mug and stood up. 'Of course. And think about what I've said.'

He could think about nothing else, about the fact that his father, not his mother, had been the guilty party all along. And it made absolute sense, of course. His father had had an endless string of women after the divorce, and they'd all been the same—blonde, busty and mindless. He'd hated every one of them.

It had been them as much as his mother that had given him his false impression of women and, of course, over the years he'd gone for the same type himself. They'd been cleverer, because otherwise they would have been too boring, but they'd all been chosen for their decorative talent and the fact that they knew the rules.

Till Fran.

Where was she now? Still in town? Was it worth combing the streets for her, or should he go to Jackie, or just wait at the gallery until she came to collect her painting?

It wasn't there any more. The exhibition had been a sell-out and had closed before Christmas, and the picture was on the wall in his study where he could sit and look at it instead of working.

He could have left it at the gallery for her to collect, of course, but he hadn't wanted to. He'd wanted it at home, so she'd have to come there to collect it, but now he wondered if she might not want to come to the house.

So he'd go there, and he'd ask Catherine yet again if she'd seen Fran, and then he'd hang about in the coffee-shop and pretend to be working and lie in wait for her.

For days, if necessary. Weeks. He could see the front of the nursing agency from the window of the coffee-shop, and he could watch it without getting cold.

His mother dropped him right outside the gallery, and as he was opening the car door she reached out and caught his hand.

'Josh?'

He turned back and her eyes searched his face, concerned. 'Good luck,' she said softly. 'Ring me.'

He nodded, unable to speak for a moment, then leant over and kissed her cheek. 'Thanks,' he said gruffly, and let himself out of the car.

She drove off with a toot and a wave, and he went into the gallery, shivering slightly in the cold wind off the river.

'Hi, Josh,' Catherine said. 'You've just missed Fran.'

'Fran?' he said, and almost stumbled.

'Careful. Lots of people fall over that mat. I think we're going to have to do something about it. Oh, and while I think about it, there's a loose door catch in the loo that could do with looking at. I don't think they've finished fixing it properly.'

'Phone Angus, take it up with him,' Josh told her. His heart was still pounding, and all he wanted to do was run outside and look for Fran, but he forced himself to be calm.

'So, when was Fran in?' he asked, trying to sound casual.

'Oh, a few minutes ago. You literally just missed her. She came to ask about her painting. I told her you'd got it at the house.'

'What did she say?'

'"Oh." Nothing else. Then she went out. She looked pale. I don't think she's very well.'

Josh nodded. 'I'm going to see if I can find her. If she comes back in, sit her down and call me on my mobile, could you? Tell her I need to speak to her.'

He went back out onto the quay and looked up and down. The light was starting to fade, but he could see a solitary figure in the distance on the path by the riverside, downstream.

Fran? It might be. He hurried towards her, his leg protesting, and as he drew closer he could see that it was her.

She was cold, standing with her arms wrapped round her waist, hugging herself miserably. She was staring out across the river, and he looked across and saw his house, the low winter sun gleaming on the windows and giving it away.

He slowed down and drew level with her, and she turned and looked at him and his heart jerked against his ribs.

Her eyes were haunted, dark circles round them, and her cheeks were sunken. She was white as a sheet, and he just wanted to gather her up in his arms and tell her it was all right.

Maybe it wasn't, though. Maybe it was nothing to do with him and there was something else wrong. The dreams again?

'Hello, Josh,' she said quietly.

'Hi. Catherine said you'd been in the gallery, and I saw you standing here. How are you?'

She shivered a little. 'Cold. I didn't realise the wind was so bitter.'

He hesitated, then went towards her and put his arm round her and led her back. 'You're freezing,' he said, feeling her thin frame trembling beneath his arm. 'You need to warm up.'

'I came to get my painting,' she said. 'I didn't realise the exhibition had finished. I'm sorry to be a nuisance.'

'You're not a nuisance. It's at my house. We could go back there now and get it, if you've got your car. We could have a cup of tea to warm you up first, if you like, or we can have something there.'

She nodded. 'There would be good,' she said, and her voice sounded hollow.

His heart ached. They walked slowly back along the river path to her car. It was parked beside the community centre, just a short distance away, and he was glad because his leg was suddenly giving him hell and he didn't fancy walking any further.

She drove him back to his house, parking a sensible distance from the garage doors, and they went inside in a brittle silence. The tension was coming off them both in waves, and he went into the kitchen and put the kettle on and started fiddling with mugs, just like his mother.

'Sit down and wrap yourself in the throw,' he told her, but she perched on the edge of the sofa and hugged herself.

'So how've you been?' she asked, finally looking at him.

'Oh, you know. Busy. The gallery's done really well.'

'So Catherine said. I'm glad for you. Were Annie and Joe pleased?'

'Yes. They asked after you. Annie sends her love.'

She'd said a lot more than that, but at the time it hadn't made sense to Josh. Now it did, and he just hoped she was right, because she'd told him he was mad to let Fran go because it was obvious she loved him.

It wasn't obvious to him, though, and he hadn't believed her—he hadn't dared to—but now, maybe, he'd find out if she was right.

He put a cup of tea down in front of Fran and she picked it up and cradled the mug gratefully. She was still shivering a little, and he turned the heating up a few degrees with the remote control, then sat back and watched her.

She looked uneasy, but he didn't know where to start, and he didn't want to risk getting it wrong again. He opened his mouth to speak, and then all the carefully prepared words vanished from his mind.

'You look awful,' he said bluntly.

Her tea slopped over the side of the mug and she put it down, her hands trembling. 'Is that supposed to be a compliment?' she said with a trace of her old spirit, and he just shut his eyes and sighed.

'I'm sorry. You look like I feel—lonely, miserable, empty. I'm lost without you, Fran,' he confessed in a ragged voice. 'I've never been lonely before, and now all I can see is the rest of my life stretching out endlessly without you, and I can't bear it.'

He opened his eyes and found she was watching him, her own eyes shimmering with tears.

'Come back to me,' he said, begging for the first time in his life, but she wasn't going to make it that easy.

'Why?' she said. 'You don't need a nurse any more.'

'No, but I need you. My life's worthless without you, and I can't go on like this.' His voice cracked, and he turned away, struggling for control. Oh, please, God, let her love me, he thought. Don't let me lose her again.

'I love you,' he said quietly. 'I think I've loved you since the moment I saw you in Jackie's agency.'

'You hated me at first.'

'No. No, I've never hated you, and I never will. I was just in pain. You were the only decent thing to happen to me, and gradually, day by day, I fell more and more in love. I was just too blind to realise it.'

'So what changed your mind?' she asked, still giving nothing away. 'You wanted me to go, the night of the private view.'

'No! No, I didn't. You wanted to go, and like a fool I let you, without telling you how I felt. And then Annie said I was mad to let you go because even a fool could see you loved me, but I couldn't see it. I hadn't seen it, because I hadn't dared to look, but I'm looking now. Tell me, Fran. Tell me how you feel, for God's sake! Put me out of my misery.'

With a low cry she threw herself into his arms and hugged him. 'Of course I love you! I thought you wanted me to go. I've missed you so much,' she sobbed, and he held her close and rocked her against his chest.

'I've missed you, too, every minute of every day. And the nights—the nights have been the worst.'

She nodded. 'I know. I haven't slept for weeks, not properly. I daren't. The dreams came back, but they were worse. You were in them, and every night—'

'Shh,' he said, hugging her closer. 'I'm here. I'm alive and I intend to be for a good long while. I'm sorry, my darling, you're stuck with me.'

'Good,' she said tearfully, and lifted her face to his. 'Take me to bed. Hold me. Be with me.'

'My pleasure,' he said gruffly, and stood up, pulling her to her feet. 'I'd carry you, but I'll probably drop you or fall. This leg's not sorted yet.'

'I think I can just about manage to walk,' she teased, but he stopped her at the threshold of his bedroom and carried her the last few strides.

'There. Now I've done it properly.'

'I thought it was after you were married you had to do that?' she said with a laugh, lying where he'd dropped her on the middle of the bed.

'Consider it done,' he said softly, and she stared at him.

'Could you rephrase that?' she said, sitting up slowly and staring at him.

Josh swallowed. Oh, hell, she wasn't going to let him get away with less, he realised. Using the edge of the bed for support, he very carefully lowered himself to his left knee and took her hand in his.

'I know I can be a miserable bastard,' he said slowly, 'and I know I've been hell to live with for the past couple of months, but I love you, Francesca Williams, and I promise I'll never give you cause to doubt me. Will you do me the honour of becoming my wife, and the mother of my children?'

She stared at him in silence for a few seconds, then a slow smile started in her eyes and spread over her face, lighting it up from inside. 'Oh, yes,' she said, laughing and crying all at once. 'Oh, Josh, yes, of course I'll marry you, you idiot, and I'll give you hundreds of kids, if that's what you want. Now, get up, you'll hurt yourself!'

He pushed up, and a stabbing pain shot through his leg, taking his breath away.

'Um—you may have to help me,' he said with a wry smile, and she slid off the edge of the bed and tucked herself under his arm, pulling up as he pushed on the bedside chest.

'You're an idiot,' she told him again, and hugged him. He just smiled. He didn't care what she called him, so long as she was there and looking at him with that light in her eyes.

He peeled off her clothes, clicking his tongue at her weight loss, then he shucked off his own things, getting the jeans trapped on the fixator in his haste.

She eased them away and then lay down beside him, her arms around him, and he went up on one elbow and kissed her. 'Just a minute,' he murmured, and turned away, reaching into the top drawer of the bedside chest. 'Here. You need this back.'

He slipped the necklace round her neck and fastened the catch, straightening it and resting the teardrop in the soft hollow of her throat. 'There,' he said softly. 'That's better. Now, where were we?'

Fran lay beside Josh, her fingers resting on the diamond, unable to believe she was there with him. He was sleeping beside her, his chest rising and falling rhythmically, and she reached up and pressed a kiss to his jaw.

His eyes fluttered open and he turned his head towards her, his eyes smiling.

'OK?' he murmured, and she nodded.

'More than OK. Wonderful.'

'Good.' The smile faded from his eyes. 'I meant it, you know,' he said quietly. 'I won't ever give you cause to doubt me. I learned today that my father is a liar and a cheat. I'll never do that to you.'

Her hand came up and cradled his cheek lovingly. 'I'm sorry. That's awful. Was that why you were so anti-marriage and -children?'

He nodded. 'Yes. My parents were a pretty grim role model, but I'll get over it. In fact, I think I pretty much have, thanks to you.'

'Good,' she said softly. 'I'll never do anything to hurt you, either, or our children. You can trust me.'

The smile returned to his eyes, and his arm tightened round her, drawing her closer as his lips found hers in a kiss full of tender promises...

If you enjoyed what you just read,
then we've got an offer you can't resist!

Take 2 bestselling
love stories FREE!
Plus get a FREE surprise gift!

Clip this page and mail it to Harlequin Reader Service®

IN U.S.A.	IN CANADA
3010 Walden Ave.	P.O. Box 609
P.O. Box 1867	Fort Erie, Ontario
Buffalo, N.Y. 14240-1867	L2A 5X3

YES! Please send me 2 free Harlequin Romance® novels and my free surprise gift. After receiving them, if I don't wish to receive anymore, I can return the shipping statement marked cancel. If I don't cancel, I will receive 6 brand-new novels every month, before they're available in stores! In the U.S.A., bill me at the bargain price of $3.34 plus 25¢ shipping & handling per book and applicable sales tax, if any*. In Canada, bill me at the bargain price of $3.80 plus 25¢ shipping & handling per book and applicable taxes**. That's the complete price and a savings of 10% off the cover prices—what a great deal! I understand that accepting the 2 free books and gift places me under no obligation ever to buy any books. I can always return a shipment and cancel at any time. Even if I never buy another book from Harlequin, the 2 free books and gift are mine to keep forever.

186 HDN DNTX
386 HDN DNTY

Name	(PLEASE PRINT)	
Address	Apt.#	
City	State/Prov.	Zip/Postal Code

* Terms and prices subject to change without notice. Sales tax applicable in N.Y.
** Canadian residents will be charged applicable provincial taxes and GST.
All orders subject to approval. Offer limited to one per household and not valid to current Harlequin Romance® subscribers.
® are registered trademarks of Harlequin Enterprises Limited.

HROM02   ©2001 Harlequin Enterprises Limited

 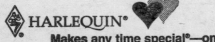

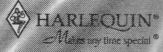